COMING HOME

COMING HOME BOOK ONE

MICHELLE ST. JAMES

BLACKTHORN PRESS

COMING HOME

Coming Home Book One
Michelle St. James

All rights reserved. No part of this book may be reproduced in any form or by any electronic means, including information storage and retrieval systems, without permission in writing from the author, except by a reviewer who may quote brief passages in review.

This is a work of fiction. Any resemblance to actual persons, living or dead, events, or locales is entirely coincidental. Any trademarks, service marks, product names, or named features are assumed to be the property of their respective owners, and are used only for reference. There is
no implied endorsement if any of these terms are used.

Copyright © 2020 by Michelle St. James
All rights reserved.
Cover design by Rebekah Zink

1

Finn Murphy opened his eyes and looked around the room, trying to remember where he was through the fog of sleep. Amsterdam? No, that had been before London. But this wasn't London either, and it definitely wasn't Indonesia or Thailand or India or Egypt or Morocco or any of the other countries he'd traveled over the past eight years.

He was in his brothers' house, and that meant he was back in Boston.

Home, or as close to one as he had.

They'd given him Declan's room and he let his gaze travel the nondescript gray walls, the functional but boring furniture, the enormous flat screen TV. Finn had been gone a long time, but to hear Ronan tell it, Declan hadn't exactly been a homebody. If he read the writing on the wall, he'd even bet Dec had been a bit of a slut before he'd reconnected with Kate Walsh.

Declan had been absent when the rest of the family had walked in on Finn in the kitchen the night before. Nick had mentioned something about Dec moving in with Kate at the Walsh estate, but it had been too chaotic to get the details, a swarm of introductions and explanations flying between him, his brothers and their spouses, and the woman named Elise who was Julia's sister and who apparently lived in the Murphy house with everyone else.

He sat up and stretched, then walked to the window in his boxer briefs. His reflection was hazy in the glass: his body corded with wiry muscle, tattoos snaking around his torso and arms, his face weather-beaten, dark beard in need of a trim.

He was almost surprised his brothers hadn't mistaken him for an intruder the night before. He was the opposite of their mostly clean-shaven faces, their quietly upscale clothes.

They looked... civilized. Normal.

The idea made him uncomfortable. If they were civilized, if they were normal, what did that make him? He pushed the question away and turned his attention to what lay beyond the window.

The view gave him a better sense of the house, two stories and shaped like a U, with a courtyard in the center underneath the window. A long patio table stood on the pavers, a couple of propane heaters at either end. Potted plants and trees dotted the patio. They were all dormant or dead now, but it was probably pretty in the summer. He could imagine his brothers and their families, sitting outside, laughing over food, talking about weddings and babies and all the other things Finn had left behind when he took off after high school.

Well, not entirely. He'd lived in a lot of places since then, had met a lot of people. In a way, his family was all over the world, a tapestry of people who had welcomed him into their homes, had broken all kinds of bread with him. He'd been to weddings in seven countries, had seen babies born in at least as many.

But it wasn't the same, although he'd worked hard to sell himself on the idea that blood family didn't matter, that family, real family, was the people you chose.

It wasn't that he didn't love his family. His father, Thomas Murphy, was a stand-up guy, an old-school Irishman who'd retired from the Boston Police Department and had never loved another woman after Finn's mother died of cancer when Finn was a kid. Finn's sister, Nora, lived in California and had worked for the FBI, although he'd heard she was doing something else now.

And his brothers, well, that was complicated. He loved them, in spite of what they did for a living. They were good men, principled in their own way, but Finn wasn't cut from the same cloth. After Erin, their youngest sister, had overdosed, Ronan, Nick, and Declan had founded Murphy Intelligence and Security.

Finn had run.

MIS had been his brothers' way of getting justice on the man who'd gotten Erin hooked on heroin in high school, the man who'd walked away when Erin died. It had started as a pact to make that man pay, a man who'd hooked countless kids like Erin on the drugs that had ruined and, in some cases, killed them. But after they'd dealt with him, they kept going, building MIS into an organization with quiet power, the kind that was used to exact justice in the shadows when the law failed.

They'd wanted to bring Finn into the organization, had encouraged him to go to school, join the military like Ronan, who'd served as a Navy SEAL, or join the Boston Police Department like Nick, who'd learned how law enforcement worked, learned how to avoid getting caught when justice didn't involve a courtroom and prison.

It had sounded crazy to Finn. Crazy and illegal, which it was. Finn hadn't wanted any part of it. To be fair, he hadn't wanted any part of anything. He'd just wanted to run — from his mother's long illness and death, from Erin's overdose, from the big house that had once been filled with laughter and noise but had become quiet as a tomb.

He hadn't planned to be gone eight years, although to be fair, he hadn't had much of a plan at all. He'd bought a used backpack, spent his graduation money on a one-way ticket to Greece, and never looked back.

Someone stepped onto the patio below the window and he leaned closer to the glass, trying to identify the figure sitting at the patio table, a steaming cup in her hands.

Not Alexa. Nick's wife had long dark brown hair. Not Julia either. Ronan's wife had dark blond hair that swung around shoulders. The figure sitting alone outside as the sun rose had blond hair that shimmered in the early morning light, long enough to be piled onto her head in a way that looked messy but somehow intentional too.

Elise, then. Julia's sister.

He'd been aware of her, standing in the kitchen, observing quietly amid all the crosstalk and ribbing and laughter that had ensued once Ronan and Nick realized the person digging around in the kitchen cupboards was Finn.

When Ronan finally introduced him to Elise, Finn had felt a moment of familiarity, like he'd met her somewhere before.

But that was impossible. He'd never seen her before in his life.

He watched as Elise sipped from the cup. He was hardly aware of digging through his backpack and pulling on his one pair of sweatpants, his eyes half on the window, hoping she wouldn't leave before he could get there.

He made his way past the closed doors in the hall and down the stairs. No one else seemed to be awake. The cavernous living room, with its two massive sectionals and big TV, was empty. The kitchen, visible from the living area, was also empty.

Chief, Ronan's dog, padded into the kitchen from her bed in the living room and sniffed at Finn's sweats.

"Hey, girl," Finn said, rubbing her short brown fur. Chief had served with Ronan in the military, and Ronan had gotten special permission to have her retired so he could adopt her. "You're getting old."

The dog licked his hand in spite of the insult.

Finn filled the dog's bowl from a container on the floor, used the Keurig to make himself a cup of coffee, then stepped out onto the patio. It was only November but it was already cold enough to see his own breath as it left his mouth.

Elise turned to look at him and he was struck by the beauty of her face — porcelain skin and high cheekbones and full lips the color of the pink tulips just past their prime he'd seen in Holland.

"Morning," she said. She was wearing a thin long-sleeved T-shirt with baggy pajama bottoms.

"Good morning." He was glad to find his voice was working. "Mind if I join you?"

"Feel free, although you might change your mind after a few minutes."

He shivered and took the seat next to her. "You aren't kidding. Want me to get you a jacket or something?"

He'd seen them hanging on hooks by the door leading to the courtyard and wished he'd grabbed one for himself too. His own short-sleeved T-shirt wasn't up to the temperature.

"I'm good," she said. "I like the cold. It wakes me up."

"I'm definitely awake." He took a sip of his coffee. "You do this often?"

"When I'm up before everyone else. It's the only time the house is quiet."

"I bet," he said. "That's quite a crew in there."

She smiled. "You say that like they're mine."

"Aren't they, in a way? You seem at home, and everyone seems to love you."

She nodded. "I am. And the feeling's mutual." He sensed something she wasn't saying, but they didn't know each other well enough to get personal. He wondered if he was imagining the shadows in her brown eyes. "What about you?"

Nice pivot, he thought. Away from her and onto him.

"What about me?"

"Seven years is a long time to be away from family," she said.

"Eight years," he corrected.

She lifted her coffee cup in a silent toast.

"It wasn't planned." He resisted the urge to spill his guts: about the way Erin's death on the heels of his mother's had leveled him, about the anger that had seeped through the house that had once been filled with love, his brothers seething with quiet rage while their father sunk into an abyss of sadness that made him seem unreachable.

She probably knew some of it anyway, but they weren't topics of conversation he'd revisited often — or ever — in the past eight years.

"And now you're back," she said.

He looked out over the empty courtyard. "Now I'm back."

"For good?" she asked.

"No." He forced down the sound of gunshots, the image of blood dripping through dirt in the mountains, the smell of gunpowder in the air.

He looked at her instead, at the haunted brown eyes, the delicate face that made him want to trace the line of her cheekbone, the thick hair he wanted to pull from the knot at the top of her head.

His heart beat faster in his chest. The flutter in his stomach was unfamiliar, but he knew well enough what it meant. Knew it wasn't good.

Not good at all.

2

Elise watched the emotion play across Finn's face and wondered what he was hiding. She wasn't one to pry — god knew she had her own secrets — but she had the feeling he hadn't come home for a simple reunion.

She didn't think she'd imagined the flash of pain behind his eyes when she'd asked if he was back in Boston for good. She wondered if it had to do with Erin, with the overdose that had shaped the rest of the Murphy siblings, sending Ronan, Nick, and Declan on a mission to exact justice for people they didn't even know, sending Nora to California, first to work with the FBI and now with Locke Montgomery's organization, a more bohemian and reckless version of MIS.

"How about you?" Finn asked. "You from Boston originally?"

"More or less," she said. "The suburbs anyway, and my gramps' cabin in the mountains."

He nodded. "Plan to stay?"

"I don't know." She looked down at the coffee cup in her hands. "Where else would I go?"

He shrugged. "It's a big world out there."

"I know." It came out sharper than she'd intended, but there was no reasonable way to tell him she'd been all over the world against her will, that the men with Manifest who'd kidnapped her and tried to traffic her had dragged her across the globe before Julia and MIS rescued her.

He nodded and stood. "I should shower and get dressed."

She'd driven him away, had been short in that way she did when someone got too close to the wounds that were still healing after two years of therapy. She could be weird with people because of what happened to her. She knew that — she just didn't know how to stop being that way.

And for some reason, she really wanted to stop being that way, at least with this man in front of her, this quiet, bearded wanderer who had appeared as suddenly as a genie out of a bottle.

"If you hurry you can be back downstairs in time for Ronan's pancakes," she said, trying to make amends.

"Ronan cooks?" He tried to imagine his big, bad brother, former Navy SEAL and resident badass, making pancakes.

"I didn't say they were good," Elise said.

He laughed. "Thanks for the warning."

She hid her smile as he stepped into the house.

Jesus... what was wrong with her? Nevermind. She knew what was wrong with her.

Trauma. PTSD.

Basically, her mind was fucked. And her heart too, in a way she couldn't explain. She'd spent the last two years working to heal from her kidnapping and abuse at the hands of Manifest. She'd done all the rights things: therapy and meditation and journaling and yoga.

But she hadn't let anyone in. Not since before. Back then she'd been a party girl, always on the move, always looking for a good time.

Julia had been the serious one, working to pay their rent when Elise couldn't come up with her half, trying to reason with Elise when she was being stupid, which was a lot of the time.

It was how Elise had gotten mixed up with Seth

MacFarland, the rich guy who'd groomed her for Manifest. She'd been easily distracted — by good-looking men who drove expensive cars and bought her Louboutins. She'd never bothered to look below the surface of anything.

That had been Julia's job. Being sensible, taking care of all the monotonous chores that made up everyday life.

But Elise had paid. Oh, how she'd paid.

Of all the things she'd lost — and she'd lost a lot — her trust in other people was the thing she missed the most. She'd been dumb. She knew that now. But she missed believing in people, missed believing they were generally good, missed having faith that she would always be okay, that she walked under a lucky star.

She missed believing in love. Missed believing someone could love her.

Who would love her now, after all that had happened to her?

The door to the house opened and she turned to see Julia step onto the patio carrying a steaming mug, a tea bag trailing from inside it.

"JT still asleep?" Elise asked. She was the only one who used the nickname for John Thomas, but it seemed like less of a burden than the name he'd been given, a name that combined the first names of the Murphy family patriarch, Thomas, and her and Julia's grandfather's name, John.

"Ronan has him," Julia said. "I figured if I came outside he might forget I exist."

"Ronan or JT?"

Julia laughed. "Both?"

Elise wasn't fooled. Julia was ecstatically happy with Ronan and the baby. That her sister had met the love of her life while searching for Elise was the one good thing to come out of Elise's kidnapping. Julia had been hunting for Elise on her own while, unbeknownst to her, their grandfather had hired MIS to look for Elise.

Julia and Ronan had literally slammed into each other in an alley behind Seth MacFarland's house, both of them casing the place for any sign of Elise.

The rest was history.

"What were you and Finn talking about?" Julia asked.

"Not much. Small talk mostly," Elise said.

"Did he say anything about why he's back?"

Elise shook her head. "Why?"

"It's just... crazy," Julia said. "He's been gone so long. Sometimes I forgot he was out there."

"Nora doesn't come home much," Elise pointed out.

"Yeah, but she has come home, and she and Braden have met up with Ronan, Nick, and Dec on jobs. Finn really did seem like a ghost. I was starting to wonder if he was real."

Oh, he's real, Elise thought, flashing to Finn's blue eyes, grayer than Ronan's and Declan's, but still Murphy blue.

What was she thinking? She didn't even like guys with beards.

"Maybe he was just ready." Even as Elise said it, she wasn't sure she bought it. The pain he'd tried to hide had been real. And who could blame him, after all that had happened in the Murphy family? All that they'd lost.

They'd each dealt with it in their own way. She couldn't fault Finn for running. Maybe it was easier to forget when you didn't have to see things that reminded you of what you'd lost.

"Maybe," Julia said. "I think something's up though. Ronan said Finn wants to take them to breakfast."

"Them?"

"Ronan, Nick, and Dec," Julia said.

Elise nodded. "I'm sure they have a lot to talk about."

"I think it's more than that. They're not going to the FT."

The Friendly Toast was their family diner spot, an eccentric diner that was so loud, the noise the Murphy family made was hardly noticed. It was great when you didn't need to talk about anything important, lousy if you did.

Elise laughed. "Not everything is a mystery."

In another life, Julia would have been a detective. Or a gossip columnist.

"Just wait. He's home for a reason. I'm going to be right about this." Julia drank from her mug. "What are you up to today?"

"I might go into the store for a bit and rack the new inventory for tomorrow. Then I have to study for finals."

She was embarrassed to say it out loud. It made her feel like a teenager, working in retail and studying for college classes. She was almost twenty-five, for god's sake. Her sister had a husband, a child. The few friends she kept in touch with on social media were either building businesses or families. Meanwhile, Elise had no idea what to do with her life, no idea what was next, what she even wanted to be next.

"Cool. Anything good come in at the store?" Julia asked.

Elise had been promoted to store manager over the summer, something she'd been proud of for about five minutes, before she remembered that Fringe, the boutique where she worked, was a one-location boutique with two employees and an absentee owner who treated the business like it was nothing more than an entertaining hobby.

"Not sure yet," Elise said. "I'll let you know after I rack the inventory."

"Awesome."

Julia had never liked shopping. That had been Elise's department, back when the men she dated had bought her handbags and shoes that cost more than the rent she'd split with Julia back when they'd had their own place.

Having Elise at Fringe to preview stock and pull aside the stuff she knew Julia would like was a perk Julia took full advantage of.

Nick's voice sounded from inside the house, followed by Ronan's, then the chime of John Thomas asking for juice.

"That's my cue," Julia said, rising to her feet. "You coming in?"

"I'll be in soon. I'm going to finish my coffee," Elise said.

"See you inside."

The voices of the people who were as much Elise's family as any she'd ever had got louder in the moment before the door closed behind Julia.

Elise finished her coffee, now cold thanks to the November air. The noise from inside the house — Julia feeding John Thomas and Alexa talking about a new contract that needed to be signed at MIS and Ronan on the phone with Declan telling him to meet them at Mike's for breakfast — made her feel like she should hurry.

Like she was running out of time. Like there was somewhere she had to be.

Except there was nowhere she really had to be, no one who was waiting for her or counting on her, but it still felt like the clock was ticking. She couldn't tread water forever.

3

Finn stepped into Mike's City Diner ahead of Ronan and Nick and scanned the space. The kitchen and counter were separated from the rest of the room by a half-wall topped with Plexiglass, the dining portion of the room filled with Formica-topped tables.

It was early for brunch on a Sunday, and at least half the tables were empty, something Finn had been counting on when he'd suggested an early breakfast. At first, he thought they'd beaten Declan to the restaurant, something that wouldn't have surprised him since, as he remembered it, Declan was almost always late.

Then a tall, broad-shouldered man stood at the back of the restaurant, his jaw shadowed with dark hair, and Finn realized with a start that it was Declan.

"There he is," Ronan said.

Declan grinned, his eyes flashing blue, and Finn hurried toward him, clasping him in a hug.

"Hey there, bro," Declan said, squeezing him. "I was beginning to think we'd never see you again."

"It's been awhile." Finn leaned back to get a look at his brother. "You grew up."

"Me?" Declan ruffled Finn's hair. "Look at you! So much for my baby brother."

Finn didn't spend much time looking in mirrors — the places he stayed weren't conducive to vanity — but he hadn't been home for eight years. He was certainly taller and more adult than he'd been when he'd left at the age of eighteen.

"It's great to see you. And you're back with Kate." Finn had gotten the short version from Ronan and Nick: Kate Walsh's return to Boston after her father's murder, the revelation that she'd been pregnant when she'd broken things off with Dec after college, the two of them finding their way back to each other.

Declan grinned. "I am." He pulled out his phone and Nick groaned as Declan tapped to a picture of a little boy with brown hair and bright blue eyes. "We have a son, Griffin."

"He definitely looks like one of us," Finn said. "I can't wait to meet him."

They took a seat and talked over each other for ten minutes while the waiter brought coffee and took their order. Finn listened as Nick told him about how he'd met Alexa, how Alexa had been working with the Attorney General's office, trying to take down MIS when they'd fallen in love.

Ronan told him about his first run-in with Julia during their work on the same case. Finn perked up when Ronan said it had something to do with Elise, then felt his heart sink when Ronan elaborated to tell him Elise had been kidnapped by an international trafficking ring run by some of the world's most powerful men.

Suddenly a lot made sense: the guarded way Elise held herself, the pain he thought he'd seen in her eyes.

He was surprised by the rage that overtook him. It was something he'd become familiar with in his travels — rage for the injustices suffered by society's forgotten, for the harm done to people and the planet by the greed of a selfish few — but it had been a long time since he'd felt such white-hot anger on such a personal level.

He hadn't even been angry when Erin had overdosed. Then he'd just been sad, emptied out by loss. But hearing what had been done to the gentle woman who'd sat with him on the patio that morning made him want to hurt someone, brought him too close to the precipice of the fury that had driven his brothers to start MIS.

"I get the feeling you're not just home for a visit," Ronan said when they were finally digging into their food.

"Coming home is a visit by definition, isn't it?" Finn tapped his fork on his plate. "But yeah, there's a reason I'm home."

"Knew it," Declan said.

"You in trouble?" Ronan asked.

Finn scowled at him. "You know me better than that."

Ronan shrugged. "I'm not sure I know you at all. It's been a long time."

The comment hurt, but Finn couldn't blame him. "I'm not in trouble. Not the way you mean."

Ronan lifted his eyebrows. "Not the way I mean?"

Finn took a drink of coffee. Damn. He'd missed American diner coffee, had missed the way it came in an endless cup and always tasted a little burnt. "I need some help, some information."

"We're listening," Nick said.

Finn was starting to understand the working dynamic between his brothers.

Ronan, a quiet giant who enjoyed the dirty work of being in the field. He wore jeans and a T-shirt, his dark hair cut close to the scalp like it had been in the military, the shadow of a beard at his jawline even though it was only ten a.m.

Nick was the thinker, the planner, wearing slacks and a crisply pressed button-down shirt even on a Sunday morning, his hair neatly styled, not too long, not too short. No surprise he married a lawyer who now worked to shield MIS from legal jeopardy.

And Declan, his blue eyes still lit with unpredictability, more refined than he'd been the last time Finn had seen him, carrying an air of sophistication that must have come with age, parenthood, or the fact that he was more or less officially part of the Walsh clan now, owners of Walsh Media Group, one of the richest companies in America.

Finn shoveled a bite of French toast into his mouth and tried to decide where to start.

"I flew in from London," he finally said, "but before that, I was staying in a little village in Ukraine, out in the country."

"Interesting," Ronan said.

Finn looked at him. "It was, actually. How I came

to be there is a story for another time, but I was staying with a family there."

"What were you doing?" Declan asked.

Finn shrugged. "Helping out on the farm, teaching some of the village kids English..."

Nick looked at him. "And?"

"And nothing." Finn bit back his annoyance. Leave it to Nick, Mr. Success, to expect Finn to be achieving something at all times.

"Did they pay you?" Nick asked.

"I didn't want money from them, and I didn't need it. But yeah, sometimes they paid me. Sometimes they made me dinner or gave me clothes," Finn said. "Agriculture is booming over there. The soil's rich, perfect for growing grain and corn."

Nick looked skeptical but Finn continued. "Anyway, this past September we were working overtime to harvest the grain, get it stored for winter and sold at market. One morning before noon I took a break with Petro, the son of the family I was staying with." An image of the boy, dark hair and brown eyes lit with mischief, filled Finn's mind. Pain swelled in his chest and he forced himself to continue. "The town was in a valley, ringed by mountains and woods. We liked to swim in one of the streams there, so we took off, planning to be back in time for lunch."

His brothers had stopped eating, their eyes riveted to Finn's face like they knew something bad was coming.

He took a deep breath. "So we went swimming, just like always, but when we got back to the house, we saw two SUVs in front of the house. We heard shouting from inside. Petro was scared." He thought of Petro's father, the warm, kind-eyed man named Fedir who had reminded Finn of his own father, and then of Fedir's wife Iryna who had delighted in stuffing him full of delicious food and doting on him like the mother Finn had lost. "These are not people who shouted at each other, so I told Petro to stay put and started for the door. But then..."

"Then?" Ronan was staring at him.

"There were gunshots. Two of them. Petro was exposed, standing there in shock, and I just... I didn't know what to do. So I got the kid and I pulled him into the trees at the edge of the house, tried to keep him quiet while a group of men left the house and got into the SUVs."

"Then what?" Ronan asked. Finn knew his brother was taking mental notes, piecing information together to solve the problem that had yet to be revealed, because he was Ronan and that's what he did: solved problems, usually by killing people.

"They drove off and I told Petro to stay hidden until I came back for him." Finn pushed his plate away, feeling sick, feeling the way he'd felt when he'd crept into the house that had been his home for the past year and a half, one of the longest stretches he'd spent in one place since he'd left Boston. "I went into the house. Fedir and Iryna — "

"Fedir and Iryna?" Nick asked.

"Petro's parents, the people who'd been letting me stay with them," Finn said. Declan nodded and Finn continued. "Fedir and Iryna were dead. Murdered."

Ronan sighed and sat back in his chair. "Fuck."

"Yeah," Finn said.

"What about the kid?" Declan asked.

"He was wrecked, obviously. I left him with his aunt and uncle and went to London," Finn said.

"Why London?" Nick asked.

"The men who'd left the house, I watched them from the trees... Most of them were soldier-types: big, wearing tactical gear. But one of them was small and spoke with an accent, British." He remembered the man's eyes, small and brown, seeming to pierce Finn's through the trees before he got in one of the black SUVs. "I thought maybe I could find something out about him."

"And did you?" Ronan asked.

Finn shook his head. "I only got a quick look at him, and I don't have the contacts to get into flight records or visa databases."

"So you have no idea who these guys are?" Ronan asked. "What about the other people in the village? What did they have to say about it?"

Finn sighed. "That's what's weird. Everybody got real quiet when I started asking questions. All these people who had been so welcoming the whole time I was there, treating me like I was one of them, closed ranks. Suddenly I was an outsider."

"You think they're hiding something?" Ronan asked.

"They're definitely hiding something," Finn said.

"Do you think they were in on it?" Nick asked.

Finn remembered the way the villagers had stopped talking to him, the way their faces, once open and excited to talk to him, had shuttered. "That's not the impression I got."

"What is the impression you got?" Ronan asked.

Finn looked at him. "That they were scared."

4

The bell on the door chimed and Elise stood up from her work and peeked around the open door of the stockroom. Her coworker, Aliyah, backed through the door of the shop, balancing her handbag in one hand and a tray holding two coffees in the other.

"Hey!" She was breathless as the door closed behind her. "It's freezing out there. I brought coffee."

"What are you doing here?" Elise asked.

"Wow, don't sound so happy to see me," Aliyah said, setting down the coffees and shrugging off her coat. Her hair was a riot of glossy curls surrounding a striking face with perfect dark skin and full lips brightened with her favorite soft pink lipstick.

Elise laughed. "I am happy to see you, just surprised. It's Sunday."

"Exactly." Aliyah touched a finger to her chin in an exaggerated Thinker pose. "And yet, here you are, working, as usual."

"I figured I'd rack that stock that came in yesterday, get a jump on the week," Elise said.

"And I figured you could use some help — and some coffee. But no hurt feelings if you'd rather be alone."

Elise knew it was true. Aliyah was the only friend she'd made since her ordeal at the hands of Manifest. It's not that she hadn't had the opportunity to make friends. There had been invites to after-class meals and study groups, but Elise always felt like there was no point. She could barely maintain the relationships she had — with her sister and her mom and the Murphys.

Aliyah had snuck up on her, their long hours at Fringe, manning the sales floor and tagging new arrivals in the stock room, providing hours of uninterrupted time to talk and laugh.

Elise hadn't meant to become her friend, but somewhere along the way it had happened anyway. Aliyah was the only person other than Elise's mom, sister, therapist, and the Murphys who knew what had happened to her.

"No way," Elise said. "I'm always happy for help, and I could definitely use the company."

Anything to keep her from thinking about her conversation with Finn Murphy, from remembering the way he'd studied her with his stormy eyes, the way he'd seemed to see all the things she tried to keep hidden.

"Cool." Aliyah handed Elise one of the coffees. "How does the new stock look?"

Elise took a drink of the coffee and headed back into the stockroom. She sat at the table and woke up her laptop, which listed all the pricing for the new stock. "See for yourself."

Aliyah flipped through the hangers on the rack. "Hmmm..."

Elise looked at her. "What?"

Aliyah shrugged. "It's not my store."

"So?" Elise sat back. She'd had her own thoughts about the store's aesthetic, thoughts that seemed best to keep to herself. She doubted Bonnie, the store's owner, would appreciate her talking smack about the stock behind her back.

"Between you and me?" Aliyah asked.

"Of course."

"It's kind of... bland. Isn't it?"

It was exactly what Elise had been thinking for the past year. "What would you do differently?"

Aliyah turned back to the rack and pulled out a white shift dress. She looked it over, put it back, and removed a black jumpsuit. "Just... add some personality, I guess? I mean, it's all well made and everything, but it's just so boring."

Elise nodded. "Numbers are down."

She was sticking to facts, trying not to editorialize in case it came back to bite her in the ass. It probably wouldn't — Aliyah was one of very few people Elise actually trusted — but she didn't want to take any chances. The job at Fringe wasn't anything special, but she enjoyed it well enough, and it was a job, a place she felt comfortable and safe.

"Maybe that's why?" Aliyah suggested. She sat down and picked up the tag gun. "Maybe Bonnie should rebrand or something. I haven't seen anyone under forty in the store in ages. Not that there's anything wrong with being over forty. But we both know young people drive trends."

"And trends leak into everything," Elise said. A woman over forty might not wear the exact same thing as a twenty-year-old, but the color and line would be impacted by what was on the runway, and that was informed by what young people wanted to wear.

"Exactly."

Elise got up to get the second tag gun and got to work at one end of the rack. Aliyah worked the other end, their unspoken plan always to meet in the middle.

Aliyah had given voice to the way Elise had started to feel about everything. In a word: bored. She was tired of living in the same place and following the same routine, of wearing the same clothes and eating the same food, watching the same shows on TV and drinking the same coffee.

She'd started craving change, color, movement. Of course, those things terrified her too. She practically broke out in hives thinking about any kind of change.

But somewhere deep in her body, in her soul, she knew she couldn't go on like she'd been doing for much longer. This wasn't what she wanted: an unfulfilling job that wouldn't even pay her bills if she wasn't living rent free with the Murphys, endless night classes, dragged out because to move forward she'd have to choose a major, actually commit to something.

The problem was, she still didn't know what she wanted. She'd had two years to figure it out, two years since her rescue from Manifest, two years of therapy and "being gentle" with herself.

At some point she had to move on.

The bell on the door rang and Elise met Aliyah's eyes.

"You didn't lock it?" Elise asked.

"I did!" Aliyah stood and headed for the door leading to the sales floor. "I'm sure I did."

Bonnie Collier walked briskly into the stock room, her Manolo Blahniks clicking on the tile.

Well, that explained the door. As the store's owner, Bonnie had a key.

"I thought I'd find you here," she said to Elise. It was barely noon on a Sunday, but Bonnie looked chic in slim gray trousers and a Fringe blouse from last season, her highlighted hair blown out into wide, loose curls, her makeup heavy but polished.

"We figured we'd get a jump on the new stock," Elise said.

Bonnie looked at Aliyah. "Perfect. It's good that you're both here."

Elise's stomach turned over. "What's up?"

Bonnie took a seat at the worktable, littered with

blank tags, Elise's laptop, and the tag guns. "Have a seat, Aliyah."

Aliyah cut a glance at Elise and sat down.

"I've sold the store," Bonnie said.

"You've... Wait, what?" Elise was almost positive she'd misheard.

"I'm sure it comes as a shock, but I couldn't say anything until it was a done deal. And now, well, now it's a done deal."

Elise tried to get her head around the revelation, the questions about what it meant for her warring with the voice inside her that had been trained to offer up socially acceptable responses. "Wow... congratulations," she finally said.

Bonnie smiled. "Thanks. I know it probably seems out of left field, but I've been wanting to streamline for a while. You know better than anyone that I'm hardly ever here, but I feel guilty when I'm not here, so..."

"I understand," Elise said. "What does this mean for the store? Will it still be called Fringe?"

"Will we keep our jobs?" Aliyah asked, cutting to the chase.

"I've sold the store to a company headquartered in the U.K. They're looking to expand here in the states and are buying up boutiques like Fringe in select cities across the country. They haven't said much about their plans, but I do know they plan to send someone in to do an audit."

Elise took a deep breath. It felt like the universe was conspiring to force her hand, pushing her out of the little nest she'd built for herself over the past two years. Finn was back in the Murphy house for who-knew-how-long, upsetting the comfortable dynamic Elise had gotten used to. She'd come to the end of her community college career and had to commit to a major if she wanted to keep going to school.

And now this.

"On the plus side, I know for a fact that they want to expand their own brand, so they're not going to turn the store into a warehouse or a fast-food joint," Bonnie said. "I've told them how invaluable you've both been to me. I don't see why they wouldn't keep you on if that's what you want."

They chatted a bit more about the transition, but Elise had a hard time focusing on the details.

If that's what you want...

That was always the problem, had always been the problem, even before Seth MacDonald had groomed her for Manifest. She'd never known what she wanted, and she wasn't any closer to knowing now.

5

Finn followed Ronan down the hall, listening as Ronan described the functions of the various rooms at MIS headquarters. Nick told him on the way over that they owned the building, occupying the entire fifth floor and leasing out just enough of the other space so as not to draw attention with a high vacancy rate.

The downtown building was both upscale and nondescript, with a cobblestone walkway that led from the street to the building and another that led from the building to a walkway on the water.

Declan had peeled off to go to his office as soon as they'd arrived. Nick stayed until they hit Alexa's office, where she was sitting at her desk, head bent to her laptop, glasses perched on her aquiline nose.

"Hey," she said when she looked up. "How was breakfast?"

"It was good." Nick walked around her desk and bent to kiss her temple, then looked at her screen. "What are you working on?"

Declan understood immediately why they'd ended up together. Alexa was gorgeous, with long dark hair and eyes like blue ice, but it was more than that. They were two wonks in the same nerd pod, off in their own world of financial data and criminal codes and all kinds of other stuff that made Finn's eyes glaze over.

Finn had been shocked to hear about the accident that had almost taken her life when she was a teenager, and about the resulting cover-up and the years of physical therapy she'd undergone to regain the use of her legs. Looking at her now, she seemed like an iron hand wrapped in a silk glove.

"Going over the standard contract, fine-tuning the wording," she said.

"Cool," Nick said. "I had some things I wanted to ask you about that."

He pulled up a chair and sat down, his eyes on Alexa's screen, Ronan and Finn forgotten.

Ronan led Finn back out into the hall and

continued to the conference room. "That's how they always are," Ronan said.

"Crazy they managed to make it work," Finn said, thinking about Alexa's former job with the Attorney General's office and the investigation of MIS that might have landed all three of his brothers in prison.

"It was touch and go for a while," Ronan said.

They passed two empty offices and Declan on the phone in another one before they reached Ronan's office.

"This is mine," Ronan said.

Finn looked around, his eyes drawn to the glass doors leading to a balcony that offered a view of the water, lapping against the concrete piling below. "Nice."

"I like it." Ronan dropped into the chair behind his desk. "Have a seat."

Finn sat in one of the chairs opposite the desk. It was weird to be in an office, surrounded by people who wore nice clothes and talked about things like contracts and office space.

"I've called in a sketch artist we've worked with in the past. She'll be able to draw a picture of the man with the British accent," Ronan said.

"Then what?" They'd steered clear of details about MIS, but Finn knew what the company did. It wasn't like they could offer up a sketch to the police and have them put out an APB.

"We'll feed it to our data guy and he'll run it through facial recognition software, see if we get a hit." Ronan hesitated. "But just so we're clear... what are you looking for here? What's your desired outcome?"

Finn already knew they were doing him a favor. Ronan had made it clear that MIS wasn't an investigative agency. Sometimes they did investigative work, but it was supposed to be part of their "core offering," which was essentially the execution of people they deemed worthy of such final punishment.

Declan was the one who'd jumped in at breakfast to remind Ronan and Nick that they'd made exceptions before, and that those exceptions had led Ronan to Julia and Nick to Alexa.

"I just want to know why," Finn said. The day was seared into his memory. Petro's excited smile as they'd made their way through the woods to the river, Finn reminding him they couldn't swim long. Their lazy walk back to the house, Petro talking excitedly in English about the frog he'd found on the riverbank. The cars parked in the dirt drive in front of the house, alarm bells ringing in Finn's ears at the sound of raised voices from inside. Gunshots. And later, after the men left, blood. "I want to know who they were, what they wanted."

"And then what?" Ronan asked.

Finn hadn't gotten that far. "I don't know. I just need to know."

Ronan nodded, but Finn could tell his big brother wasn't happy. "Just promise me you're not going to go off half-cocked."

"Shouldn't I be the one asking for that promise?" Finn asked.

Ronan's eyes flashed and Finn instinctually braced himself for Ronan's wrath. As the oldest and biggest, Ronan had put the fear of god into all of them as kids, except maybe Declan, who'd had more hubris than good sense even then.

Thomas Murphy had believed in letting his boys work out their own problems, that a little scuffle on the front lawn, a bloody nose or two, never hurt anyone. But Finn's mother had softened his father before her death, and Finn had been surprised to find his father further softened after it, as if he knew she was watching and was trying to make her happy even in the afterlife.

"We're a business," Ronan said. "We don't go off half-cocked. We take cases based on facts, and we execute them according to our clients' wishes. You're the client."

"I'm not hiring you to hurt anyone," Finn said.

"I know that's true right now." Ronan hesitated. "I also know how things can change once anger and a need for justice have a focal point."

"I'm not like you." Finn tried to keep the words even as he bit them out through clenched teeth. He didn't want to start something, especially not with Ronan. It wasn't Finn's style. He preferred to avoid conflict, to avoid anything that cut too deep, that got too close to the truth of his feelings.

It was why he'd run all those years ago after Erin's overdose, why he'd stayed away. It was obvious his family was cursed. He had no desire to stick around and be reminded of all they'd lost, and even less desire to wait for another shoe to drop.

Ronan didn't say anything, but Finn could tell he'd hit a nerve by the way Ronan's jaw clenched, the way he straightened in his chair. "Good, then we'll see what the facial recognition turns up and you can put this all to bed."

It sounded good to Finn. Find out what had happened in Ukraine, ease the questions that had kept him up at night in the weeks since Fedir and Iryna's murder, take the next flight out of Boston.

It's not like he had any reason to stay.

6

"You sure you're okay with me driving?" Elise asked Finn as they left the house.

He shrugged. "Doesn't matter to me."

The smell of roasting turkey and pumpkin pie wafted through the courtyard. Elise tucked her chin into her coat, feeling unusually content. Almost everyone she loved was inside the house, cooking and laughing and bickering over Thanksgiving preparations, the cold weather only adding to the house's sense of safety. Thomas Murphy was even there, and Lisa, Julia and Elise's mother.

Plus, there was him. Finn.

They left the courtyard and walked toward the Audi parked out front. It was Julia's, but it might as well have been Elise's considering how much she drove it. She hadn't had the money to buy her own car, and no way would she take money from Julia, even though Julia and Ronan were loaded and had offered. Somehow borrowing the car all the time didn't seem on par with taking money to buy her own.

"Did they text you the list?" Elise asked, getting behind the wheel.

Finn pulled his phone from his pocket the way he always did, like he was surprised to find it there. He hadn't had a phone during the eight years he'd traveled the world, one of many things he'd told her in the weeks he'd been back in Boston. He'd only agreed to get one now because it made it easier for Ronan, Nick, and Declan to contact him about the case they were working for him.

"Yep," he said.

"Cool."

She started the car and they pulled out into the street. Traffic was light, most of the city already sitting around a Thanksgiving table, and she navigated through the mostly empty streets as a familiar silence settled between them.

It wasn't entirely comfortable. They'd spent a fair

amount of time together since he'd settled into the house — making food with the rest of the family, sitting on the sofa with takeout while they all watched their favorite reality TV shows.

But they hadn't spent much time alone, something that had been intentional on Elise's part. It had been so long since she'd felt a pull of attraction to any man, she almost hadn't recognized it when it hit her. Once she realized what she was feeling — the nervous stomach and excited flush she always felt in his presence, the extra attention she paid to her appearance when for two years she'd made a point not to draw attention to herself — she'd made a promise to herself to squash it. Her life had gotten complicated enough, especially with the store being sold.

The last thing she needed was the complication of Finn Murphy, but now she couldn't help wondering if she was imagining the chemistry zinging between them in the car.

He was so close she could almost feel his proximity in the air, a primal vibration her own body was all too happy to receive. His thighs strained at the fabric of his jeans, his chest stretching his white T-shirt, his arms lean but muscular. She'd spent too much time trying to ignore those arms over the past couple of weeks, trying not to wonder what they would feel like wrapped around her.

He smelled like soap and something subtle that might have been aftershave, although he hadn't shaved his beard.

She was relieved when she spotted the grocery store up ahead. Being alone in a car with Finn suddenly seemed like a bad idea.

"Are they closed?" Elise asked, peering at the grocery store through the windshield as they pulled into a nearly empty parking lot.

"Not for another half hour," Finn said from the passenger seat. "I checked before we left the house."

She put the car in park and smiled at him. "So you admit having a smart phone is helpful."

"I wouldn't say helpful," he hedged. "Let's just say it has its moments of convenience."

"Ha. I knew it," she said, reaching for the door handle.

She was careful to keep distance between them, her hands stuffed in her pockets, as they hurried into the store.

She grabbed a basket. "What's on the list?"

He held up his phone, forcing her to step closer

to get a look at the text: lemon, celery, butter, heavy cream.

She memorized the list so she wouldn't have to lean in again. "Let's go."

They headed for the produce section.

"Is it always like this?" Finn asked.

Elise threw a bunch of celery into the basket. "Is what always like what?"

"Thanksgiving. Is it always crazy and noisy and... chaotic?"

"Have you met your family?"

He grinned, and her knees felt weak. He didn't smile much, but when he did... god help her. "Not recently."

"Well, the short and dirty version is that there's a lot of them, and they like to talk, and they're super opinionated. There are three big men who like to argue and who are still playing out their childhood sibling rivalry. Also, there are two kids. One of them whines and cries when he's tired and hungry and the other wants someone to play video games with him 24/7."

"Haha," Finn said. "How many lemons should I get?"

"Um... four?" She was guessing. She didn't

remember a number on the list and she wasn't about to lean in for another look.

He put the lemons in the basket. "Do you mind it?"

"The noise and stuff?" she asked. He nodded, and she thought about the question. "Most of the time I find it comforting. There's always someone around to talk to or watch TV with. You're never alone."

"What's the downside?" he asked as they continued toward the store.

"You're never alone," she said.

He laughed and she bit her lip to keep from smiling. She needed him to stop doing that. The smiling. The laughing. The being charming and interesting and so blindingly attractive.

They reached the dairy case and she scanned the shelves for the butter. "Did you miss it?"

"It was different when I left," he said. "It was me, Dec, and our dad. Ronan had joined the military, Nick was working for Boston PD, Nora had gone off to school. We weren't close."

"Really?" She couldn't help being surprised. The three other Murphy brothers fought plenty, but she'd sensed a deep respect and affection between them.

He nodded. "It was kind of grim, to be honest. That's part of why I left."

She grabbed a carton of heavy cream and put it in the basket. "Are you surprised things are so different?"

"Yes and no."

This was good. She could keep him talking, focus on what he was saying and not how he looked in those jeans, not the piercing blue eyes that she'd never thought twice about on Ronan or Declan. "How so?"

"It's different, but your sister is pretty amazing. And so is Alexa and Kate."

"You think that's what made the difference?" she asked.

"I can't think of anything else. Believe me when I say I never in a million years would have imagined Ronan cooing over a kid and trying to cook," he said.

"Trying being the operative word." Ronan had been trying to learn to cook since Julia had been pregnant with John Thomas. That he hadn't improved was a source of

bafflement by everyone in the house.

"True. He made me an omelet the other day. The outside was brown and dry and the inside was raw."

"Sounds like one of Ronan's omelets." She held up the basket. "This is it, right?"

"Yep."

"Good. I'm starving," Elise said.

They started down one of the aisles, heading for the front of the store. They'd just turned the corner when Elise stopped in her tracks.

The man walked toward her, strands of silver shining in his dark hair. He was middle-aged, with the confident walk and trim physique of someone who might have been in the military.

Her heart pounded in her chest, blood rushing to her head, making her feel flushed and faint. She was only vaguely aware that she was no longer holding the basket with their groceries, that everything had tumbled out around her feet.

"Hey... what is it? Are you okay?" It was Finn's voice, coming at her as if down a long tunnel, her vision growing black around the edges, like she might pass out.

But she couldn't pass out. If she passed out, they could do anything to her. She wouldn't be able to stop them. She wouldn't even know what they did.

She had to stay awake, had to fight against the drugs they pumped into her veins to keep her compliant.

She shrugged off Finn's arms and he backed away, held up his hands. "It's okay. It's me." He took a step toward her. "I'm going to take your hand and we're going to walk out of here, okay?"

She flinched when he took her hand, but somewhere in the murk of her mind she knew it was him.

Knew she was safe.

"Let's go," he said. "I've got you. I've got you."

7

Finn opened the car door and closed it behind Elise, then worked to compose himself as he started for the driver's side. He didn't know what had happened back there, but she had obviously been terrified, and her fear had stirred up a storm of emotion inside him that he couldn't begin to name.

He slid into the driver's seat and closed the door. He turned to look at her and found her staring down at her hands, tears streaming down her cheeks.

He wrapped his hands around the steering wheel to keep from touching her, the last thing she would want given her reaction in the store.

"What happened? Is there someone in there? Someone you're afraid of?" he asked.

"Yes... No..." She inhaled a deep shuddering breath. "I don't know. I think I imagined it."

"Can you tell me?" He tried to keep his voice even, hoped she couldn't hear the emotion coursing under it.

"A couple of years ago, something happened to me." She turned her face to the window. "You probably already know."

"I know some of it." He continued, not wanting her to feel that her privacy had been violated. "None of the details."

She looked down at her hands. It was a gesture he was beginning to recognize, one she used when she didn't want him to look too closely at her.

Problem was, he couldn't stop looking at her.

"I'm mostly okay," she said. "It's just... sometimes I see someone who looks like one of the men and —"

He sat up straighter, his eyes on the store. "In there?"

"It was just a guy. It's always just a guy. But sometimes they have the same hair or the same walk or the same eyes and I just... freeze. I don't know if it's because the man who groomed me was from Boston or if it's something I would have to live with no matter where I lived, but when it happens I feel like..."

"Like?" he asked softly.

"Like I'm going to pass out. Like I'm coming apart. Like... my insides are going to overflow my body, like I'm not in control of it at all." She looked at him. "I'm sorry. This is intense."

He shook his head. "You have nothing, absolutely nothing, to be sorry for. I don't know how anyone can ever be okay after something like that." He had to fight to keep the anger out of his voice. Anger wasn't what she needed. "I think you're incredibly strong to be doing so well."

She laughed but there was no humor in it. "I'm not doing well. I'm not doing anything."

"What makes you say that?" he asked.

"I'm just treading water," she said. "I've been doing the exact same thing for two years. And you want to know the worst part?"

He nodded.

"I'm no closer to figuring it out now than I was two years ago, when your brothers brought me back to Boston. I have no idea what I want my life to look like."

He didn't think about reaching for her hand. He

just did it. Just wrapped his hand around hers, wanting to show her she wasn't alone.

"I'm sorry." He went to pull his hand away and was surprised when she held it tighter.

"No... it's nice." She hesitated. "Except for the occasional hug from Ronan or Nick or Dec, I haven't been touched by anyone but Julia in... well, a long time. Unless you count John Thomas drooling and smearing his sticky fingers all over me."

"I would not count that, no." He thought about what she'd said. "There's no rush you know."

Her hazel eyes met his through the darkness between them, the flecks of green he sometimes saw swimming in them catching what little light shone into the car. They were eyes he could get lost in, a mystery he could spend a lifetime trying to solve.

"What do you mean?" she asked.

"You said you were no closer to figuring it out, to knowing what you wanted. But you have all the time in the world. There's no rush."

She smiled. "Says the guy who's been aimlessly roaming the world for eight years."

He returned her smile. "Says that guy."

"It's just hard. Everyone else seems to know what they want. No one's pressuring me or anything, but your brothers have MIS. Julia helps out with the company's network security, but she also has John Thomas. Alexa is... well, Alexa." She laughed. "She was a success story even before she met Nick. Same with Kate, who I'm pretty sure is going to run the world someday from her office at Walsh Media Group."

"They're not you. They're not me." Since when was he aligned with Elise Berenger? Since when were they on the same team? "And the thing is, they're happy doing what they do. That's what I want, and it's what you deserve. I'd rather wander for another ten years than choose something just to choose something, just to fit into someone else's idea of a successful life. Isn't the point to be happy?"

She nodded. "I think so. That's what I hear anyway."

He laughed a little and squeezed her hand. It felt good in his. Like maybe it belonged there. Like maybe he'd been waiting for it a long time. "Same."

She looked at him and the moment seemed to stretch taut between them, filled with words neither of them had and feelings they hadn't yet defined. "Thanks."

"For what?"

"For listening. For helping me in there." She

looked at the store through the windshield. "They're closing. We didn't get the groceries."

"Don't worry about that. We'll find another market."

"Can we keep this between us?" she asked.

"Of course, but I hope you know it's nothing to be ashamed of," he said. "It's okay to feel things."

She drew in a breath and nodded. "I know. I just don't want to worry Julia. She's done so much to make sure I'm okay. If it wasn't for her and Ronan..." Her voice trailed off. She shook her head, an iron wall dropping over her eyes. "I don't like to think about what might have happened to me, about where I'd be right now."

Pulling her toward him was pure instinct. The need to comfort her, yes, but the desire to protect her too. To make her feel safe.

He half-expected her to pull away. Instead she sank into him. Against his will, his body responded to her warmth, the smell of her shampoo — vanilla and coconut — mingling with the scent of her skin.

"You're safe now," he said. "We're not going to let anyone hurt you ever again."

He wondered if she caught his use of the pronoun "we," wondered when he'd begun to think of himself on the same team as his brothers, at least when it came to protecting Elise.

A wave of panic rolled through him. His trip to Boston was meant to be a quick one, its purpose to find answers about the men who had killed Fedir and Iryna, for Petro and for his own sense of closure.

Spend a little time with the family, see what he could find out about what had happened in Ukraine, and get back on the road before he could get sucked into a life he didn't want.

That was the plan. He couldn't allow anything to pull him off course — not even Elise Berenger.

8

Elise flipped through the rack of blouses at the back of the store, making sure they were lined up according to size.

"No one's come in since you did that last," Aliyah said from behind the counter.

"And you're not even on the schedule today, so don't act like I'm the only one who's crazy," Elise said.

Aliyah laughed. "Touché."

They were waiting for Fringe's new manager to make an appearance, the first time they would meet him since Bonnie had sold the store. In anticipation, Elise had gotten to work early, making a careful pass of the store, straightening hangers and sweeping the floor and cleaning the already spotless store windows.

Now it was almost lunch time, and William Pearson still hadn't made an appearance.

"Did you Google him?" Aliyah asked.

"Of course," Elise said. "Didn't you?"

Aliyah laughed. "Duh. He's cute, right?"

Elise shrugged. "He's okay."

In the pictures online, he looked like every other young successful guy in a suit, his hair short and neatly groomed, his teeth perfectly straight and white in the homogeneous way of all people who'd had braces. His face was narrow, his features perfectly symmetrical, like they'd been carved by a 3-D printer from a series of specifications for the perfect man, something that ironically made him less perfect, at least in Elise's eyes.

"He's single," Aliyah sang out.

Elise flashed to Finn's face — his piercing eyes, the jaw almost too strong, lips almost too full, hair still a bit long, beard trimmed ever so slightly since he'd been home but still wild.

Something had shifted between them in the week since Thanksgiving. Something subtle but seismic. It wasn't what she'd expected after her freak out in the grocery store. She'd gotten used to hiding the scary parts of herself. What had happened to her made people uncomfortable. They didn't know what to say but they thought they should say something, so they usually said a bunch of expected stuff (*I'msorry/That'ssoawful/I'msogladyou'reokay*) and then avoided her after that.

She didn't blame them. What could they say? And if there was nothing to say, how could they be her friend? How could anyone ever be more than that?

But Finn hadn't avoided her. If anything, he seemed to seek her out more often. Their conversations had gotten longer and more rambling, covering everything from his experiences on the road to her childhood with Julia and their grandfather, who'd hired MIS to find Elise and then been murdered by Manifest.

He didn't push for details about what had happened to her, but he didn't seem afraid of them either.

"Ugh, no. That's the last thing I need," Elise said to Aliyah. "I can't even date people outside of work."

"Exactly. Which might be why the universe is about to drop a successful hottie right into your lap."

The bell on the door chimed and Elise turned

toward the front of the store in time to see William Pearson step inside.

He strode into the showroom like he'd been there a thousand times before. In a way, he probably had. According to the research Julia had done (there were advantages to having a sister who used to be a digital investigator), Pearson was Vice President of North American Acquisitions for Mirage Holdings.

Elise could only guess the bulk of his job involved days like this one, days spent paying visits to little stores like Fringe that had been gobbled up by Mirage, looking for ways to make it compliant with their brand by eliminating everything that made each store unique.

"Good morning." Elise approached him with an outstretched hand. "You must be William Pearson. I'm Elise Berenger."

He shook her hand and held her gaze. His eyes were a more complex shade of brown than they'd appeared online, his features more refined.

"Good morning." His British accent was crisp. "It's a pleasure meeting you."

His gaze combed her face, and she had the sense that she was being catalogued for later reference. It wasn't a pleasant sensation.

She turned to look at Aliyah. "This is Aliyah Aldridge, our Assistant Manager."

Aliyah came around the counter and shook William's hand. "Nice to meet you."

"You as well."

His eyes skipped away from Aliyah's face. He scanned the store, and Elise had that sense again: that he was processing, his brain a computer that was already making notes on merchandising and stock.

He looked at Elise. His eyes were empty. "Right. Show me around then."

"Of course."

She caught Aliyah's raised eyebrows as she passed, leading him to the back of the showroom. Elise explained the inventory and layout, elaborating on their stock and the characteristics of their typical customer.

He said very little, just nodded from time to time as she detailed everything she thought he might want to know and answered the few questions he asked.

She explained their point of sale system and continued into the stock room where she outlined their methodologies for keeping track of incoming stock, damaged items and other manufacturer returns, and items slated to be shipped from purchases on the little-used Fringe website.

"Very orderly," he said when she was done. It almost sounded like a compliment, but his icy demeanor made it hard to be sure.

"Most of it was set up by Bonnie," she said. "You can let us know what you'd like changed. Obviously, it's your call now."

"And you?"

"Me?" It was such an abrupt change of conversation she didn't have time to formulate a more intelligent response.

"Will you be staying on?" he asked.

She smiled. "I suppose that's your call too."

He held her gaze, and she had to hold her body rigid in an effort to resist a shiver. "You're right, of course."

The coldness of the proclamation, the appraising look in his eyes, made her feel like she was nothing more than inventory, something for him to keep or cast aside depending on his mood.

She knew that look. Knew what it felt like to be weighed and measured, assessed for value. It wasn't about the store or her job as manager. There was something else in his eyes, something that managed to be both too intimate and faintly cruel.

He walked past her, set his bag on the stockroom table, and unpacked his laptop without looking at her. She thought he might say something else, something to soften the harshness of his words. When it became apparent he had nothing else to say, she turned and left the room, taking a deep breath before stepping back into the showroom.

Aliyah looked up from her position at the checkout counter and mouthed the words, "Oh my god."

Elise could tell from the excitement in her eyes that Aliyah didn't mean it in a bad way, and since there was no way to explain the ice that had seeped through her veins when William Pearson had looked at her in the stockroom, especially not with him still in the store, she shook her head and moved toward one of the mannequins against the wall.

She'd just changed the outfit the day before, wanting to make sure everything displayed was from new stock, or as fashionable as it could be at Fringe. But she was filled with nervous energy, the need to do something with her hands, something that would keep her away from Aliyah while she tried to talk herself down from what was just another panic attack triggered by a perfectly normal conversation with the person who would decide her fate at Fringe.

He wasn't exactly Mr. Warmth, but that didn't mean he was a psychopath.

She was removing the mannequin's scarf when her phone pinged inside her pocket. She glanced back at the stockroom to make sure William was still there, then looked at her phone.

It was a text from Finn.

What are you doing after work?

Her heart beat faster, and she knew her face was flushing from the heat that rose to her cheeks. **Nothing. Why?**

She didn't have to wait long for a reply.

Want to meet me somewhere?

She smiled down at her phone. **Can you be more specific?**

I'd rather it be a surprise. 7pm?

What was this? A date? A friend thing? An errand for Julia or Ronan?

She texted fast, before she could change her mind. **Okay.**

Wear loose, comfortable clothes and meet me on the corner of Melcher and A Street. See you then.

Loose comfortable clothes? What the...?

She closed her phone and slipped it in her pocket. She took a deep breath as she went back to work, trying to place the feeling in her stomach, in her chest.

Was she scared? Nervous?

No. Neither of those things was right. She was going to do something with Finn, something that might not be a date but definitely wasn't an errand either.

And she was excited.

9

Finn held the door for Elise and they stepped onto the sidewalk, surprisingly busy with pedestrians given the hour. The cold air hit the sweat on his body like a bucket of ice, and he paused to zip up his jacket, glad Elise was wearing a heavier coat.

They walked a couple of minutes in silence. He was beginning to think he'd made a mistake when she took his hand and stepped out of the flow of walking traffic.

"That was... wow," she said.

"Was it okay?" he asked. "I didn't want to be presumptuous, but I met this guy once in Amsterdam, a doctor who does trauma research. He'd told me it's not all in the mind like they say, that some of it is stored in the body, which is why PTSD elicits a physical response like your panic attack at the store." He shook his head. "I'm sorry. You probably know all of this."

"I've heard it before, but I never did anything about it." Darkness passed over her eyes like a storm cloud. "I haven't... I haven't been very in touch with my body since I've been back."

She blushed and he had to resist the urge to lean over and tuck the piece of golden hair that had come loose from her ponytail behind her ear.

"That's understandable," he said. "I got into yoga when I was in India. I don't have trauma like yours — " She opened her mouth to object, probably because she knew about his mother, about Erin. But this wasn't about him. "No, it's not the same. But I have found yoga to help in just... releasing some of that shit, you know?"

She nodded. "I do know."

"Anyway, I hope it was okay. I just thought it might help, and I... well, I want to help, Elise. If that's okay, I mean."

He felt like an idiot. A stupid, fumbling idiot saying all the wrong things, doing all the wrong things, too aware of the fact that she was still holding his hand, that they were standing only inches apart, that the sweat from her body smelled tangy and sweet.

Too aware of the fact that this was a mistake even if it felt like the most right thing to happen to him in a very long time, even if their paths were destined to diverge.

"It's more than okay. I feel... lighter," she said. He'd seen the tears streaming down her face during the class and had looked away, not wanting to make her feel self-conscious. "It was a really nice thing to do. Thank you."

"You're welcome. I'm glad it was the right thing." He hesitated. He didn't want to make any of this about him, didn't want her to reassure him. "I haven't been around people much for the past few years. Ukraine was the longest I've stayed in one place. I don't always know what to say or do to make things better for you, but I want to try. Just promise me something?"

"Sure."

"Tell me if I'm an idiot. If I say or do the wrong thing?"

She laughed. "I can't imagine that."

He grinned. "Then you suffer from a serious lack of imagination. Hey... are you hungry?"

He almost held his breath. The yoga was one

thing — she hadn't known what she was getting into, and he'd wanted to help as a friend if nothing else. Dinner was more clearly in date territory, even post-yoga.

She didn't hesitate. "I'm starving actually. Apparently getting rid of toxic feelings works up an appetite."

He liked her. He really liked her.

Of course, he liked the way she looked. That was a no-brainer, although he tried not to linger too long on thoughts of her willowy limbs and long neck, her delicate features and big eyes, the flaxen hair he could too easily imagine streaming across his pillow.

But it was more than that. He liked her easygoing nature, the way she said what was on her mind even when it was awkward. He liked her humor, the way she could find something to laugh about even when they were having a heavy conversation.

"Agreed," he said. "I know an amazing taco place around the corner, if it's still there."

"Tacos sound perfect."

He didn't let go of her hand as they stepped back onto the sidewalk. He was already looking forward to dinner, to sitting in a warm restaurant with Elise across from him for a whole hour.

His phone buzzed from inside his pocket.

"It's Ronan." He held the phone to his ear. "Hey. What's up?"

"We got something," Ronan said. "From the sketch and facial recognition search."

Finn slowed his steps, aware of Elise's curious gaze. "Did you find him?"

"It's... more complicated than that," Ronan said. "Can you come to the office?"

"I'll be there in twenty minutes."

"What is it?" Elise asked when he disconnected the call.

"They got something on that sketch." He'd told Elise about what happened in Ukraine. She knew why he'd come home, knew about the sketch and the man MIS was trying to identify. "I'm sorry. I have to go to the office."

"It's totally fine."

He could tell she meant it. "I'll walk you to the car."

He'd been borrowing one of Nick's or Ronan's vehicles, depending on which car was free.

"Can I come with you?" she asked.

"To the office?"

She nodded. "I won't be offended if you say no. I just..." She bit her lip. "I want to help you too. I can't do anything about the man who hurt your friends, but I'd like to be there for moral support. If that's okay, I mean."

Part of him didn't want her there. That part wanted to keep her from everything ugly. She'd seen enough ugly. That part of him wanted to show her only beauty, only healing, only love.

But he also wanted to keep her with him as long as possible. Was it a desire for the moral support she was offering? Lust? Something deeper than lust?

He didn't know. He only knew that he wasn't ready to be apart from her just yet.

"Of course it's okay. I'll follow you to the office."

"I parked on the next block," she said.

They continued to the car, Finn's thoughts torn between the news he was about to receive from Ronan and the fact that he liked Elise Berenger too much.

Way too much.

10

Elise had been at MIS more times than she could count, but not like this. She'd always come on her way to somewhere else, dropping something off for Julia or picking up John Thomas so Julia could get more work done.

Now she saw it all through the eyes of the people who hired them. The lobby was empty and quiet, furnished with gray carpet, two chairs Elise had never seen occupied, a couple of potted plants, and a coffee table featuring two neat stacks of magazines Elise would bet no one had ever read.

Reilly — she thought his first name was Mark — manned the front desk, his suit jacket bulging with the weapon Julia had told her Reilly carried as part of his joint greeter/security role for MIS.

"They're in the conference room," he said as she and Finn stepped out of the elevator.

"Thanks," Finn said.

They continued down the hall, past the offices used by Alexa and Nick, past Ronan's office and a little kitchen she doubted anyone used for more than making coffee.

It was mostly a ruse, the office designed to look like what the Murphy brothers wanted it to look like — a high-end investigative and security firm hired by affluent clients to dig up dirt on professional opponents, provide countermeasures for companies concerned with corporate espionage and security for those with executives traveling to political hot spots around the world.

She knew from Julia that they took on a handful of these clients to maintain the appearance of a legitimate business, knew that Nick was meticulous in keeping the books — and paying taxes — in such a way that the IRS would never have a reason to dig into the company's financials.

Ronan and Nick were already at the conference table when she and Finn entered the room. She registered the surprise on Ronan's face when he saw Elise with Finn and wondered if she was imagining his pinched smile.

"Hey," Finn said.

Ronan nodded. "Thanks for coming so fast. We're still waiting for Dec."

"We weren't far," Finn said.

Elise waited for him to elaborate. When he didn't, she removed her coat and rubbed her hands together. "I'm going to make tea. Can I get anything for anybody else?"

"I'll take a coffee," Nick said.

She didn't have to ask how he took it. No one had been more surprised than her by her close friendship with Nick. Julia had been worried about it at first, had thought there was more than friendship between them, but it had never been that way between her and Nick, even before he'd met Alexa.

She and Nick had just clicked, like friends who'd known each other forever. She'd talked to him about what happened to her at the hands of Manifest, and he'd told her everything about his feelings for Alexa before word had gotten out to the rest of the family that Nick was in love with the attorney who planned to send them all to jail.

Elise left the room nursing second thoughts. Maybe she shouldn't have come. Maybe it would send the wrong signal to Ronan, Nick, and Dec about her relationship with Finn, a relationship that was... what exactly?

The yoga might have been a gesture of friendship, but Finn had invited her to dinner afterwards, and she didn't think she was imagining their physical attraction, the chemistry that filled the empty space between them until she could almost feel his hands on her even though they'd never done more than hold hands.

She pushed the thought away. It was too much. Too much to consider, too much to figure out, right now. She would let the brothers say whatever they needed to say to each other about it and leave it at that.

She made her tea and Nick's coffee and returned to the conference room.

"Dec's still not here?" She passed the coffee to Nick and sat next to Finn.

"Are you surprised?" Nick asked.

"I guess not," she said.

"Why does Dec have to be here?" Finn asked, shifting in his chair and tapping his fingers on the conference table. "Just tell me what they found."

"That's not how we do things," Ronan said.

"I'm not a client," Finn said through gritted teeth.

"You're not a paying client," Ronan said. "But we

treat every client — even the ones who don't pay — like paying clients. It's good business."

Elise knew what he meant. Nick's financial management wasn't the only mechanism in place to protect the business and the family. There were things like this — a meticulous attention to detail, the careful attention paid to not getting lazy.

There were other things too: offshore bank accounts and properties all over the world owned by shell companies owned by the Murphys and fake passports in case they had to run.

For Elise too.

They'd made her part of their family, and while she didn't know everything that went on at MIS, she'd accepted the risks as part of the package. She trusted them, knew they'd taken every precaution to ensure she, Julia, John Thomas, Alexa, and Declan's family would be able to get out if the worst happened.

"Declan has to be here if we talk about next steps," Nick clarified. "Everything we do is unanimous."

"Sorry I'm late," Declan said, entering the room.

Once upon a time, Declan being late wouldn't have raised an eyebrow. He was the second-youngest Murphy brother, but whether because Finn had been gone for so long or as a product of his personality, when Elise had met him, he'd been the resident fuckup, getting into bar fights and bringing home a different girl every night.

Then a case at MIS had reconnected him with Kate Walsh, his college sweetheart, and he'd found out they shared a son. After that he got his act together fast, a necessity if he wanted to prove he was worthy of Kate, who was pretty much an icon in the business world.

"Let's get started," Ronan said, ignoring the apology. Declan had stepped up, but that didn't mean the brothers would cut him any slack, any more than they'd expect to be cut slack themselves. Ronan looked at Nick. "Hit the lights, will you?"

Nick stood and crossed to the light switch while Ronan reached for the laptop in front of him.

An image of the sketch appeared on the screen hanging on the wall behind Ronan. Elise hadn't seen it, but she knew from Finn that it had been drawn based on his recollection of the British man who'd been present when Finn's host family in Ukraine had been murdered.

The sketch depicted a man with a narrow face and pinched features. His eyes were small, and she thought she saw something calculating in them, although she knew that might be projection on her part. His hairline was receding, creating a widow's peak of thin brown hair.

"The sketch gave us five hits initially," Ronan said.

"Five?" Finn sounded surprised.

"It's a sketch," Ronan said. "We sent it through a program that searches billions of faces. It's a miracle it was that low."

Finn nodded, conceding the point, and Ronan continued. "We were able to rule out two of them right away."

"How did you rule them out?" Finn asked.

"One of them was at a conference in Switzerland at the time of the Ukrainian incident," Nick said.

Finn looked at him. "The murder, you mean."

Nick nodded.

"The other one uses a wheelchair," Ronan said. "He's had advanced MS for years."

"What about the other three?" Finn asked.

"We can't rule them out," Ronan said. "Which is why we needed you here." He tapped a key on the laptop and the sketch was replaced by a full color image that looked like a corporate headshot, something featured in an annual report or on a website. "This is Ronald Wellick. He works for a multinational finance firm, trades in commodities. There are no red flags in his background, but that can be said about all three of the men who came up as matches to the sketch. Since Clay wasn't able to verify Wellick's whereabouts on the date of the murders, we decided to keep him in the running."

Clay was the tech wiz who headed up MIS' digital operation. He was an independent contractor, but Elise guessed he knew the truth about MIS. She'd only met him a couple of times in the office, and she'd been surprised by how small and young he looked, especially after Julia told her he used to be an analyst for the NSA.

"The face ring a bell?" Declan asked Finn.

Elise watched Finn's face as he studied the image on the screen.

He shook his head. "Not really. There's a resemblance, but I can't be sure it's him."

Elise didn't blame him. The guy on the screen looked just enough like the sketch to make it possible they were the same man but not quite enough to call him an exact match. She wondered if that would be true of the other two men who'd come up as matches.

"Let's move on," Ronan said. "See if one of the other two look more familiar."

The image on the screen changed to that of another man. This image was candid, a man walking outside on a busy street, other pedestrians in both directions. His body was hidden by a long coat, but his face was turned toward the camera, his features clear and close enough to the sketch to be jarring, even for Elise who'd never seen the man in the flesh.

"Oliver Paine," Ronan intoned. "Works for a boutique hospitality company. Can't find any obvious connection to Fedir and Iryna, but his grandparents immigrated to Wales from Russia, so we figured it was worth a shot."

"They look like the same person," Finn said. "What about his whereabouts on the date of Fedir and Iryna's murder?"

"This is the part that's weird," Ronan said. "He was in Croatia, on a work trip to preview a hotel his company's building there."

Finn's expression gave nothing away. "Not exactly a hop, skip, and a jump from Croatia to Ukraine."

"No, but not impossible either."

Finn leaned back in the chair and tugged on his beard. "True."

"Last one." Ronan cued up the next image. This one was a man in a tweed jacket, standing at the front of some kind of lecture hall, a screen behind him displaying a series of symbols and numbers Elise couldn't begin to decipher. "This is Isaac Fleming. A geologist."

"A geologist," Finn repeated.

"I know," Ronan said. "It's a long shot. But he was one of the hits, and since for all intents and purposes, you're the client here, it's not for us to edit the information that comes back from Clay. Also, the security system at the lab where he works didn't log him in on the day of the murders."

"Is that a pattern?" Declan asked. "Does he miss work often?"

"I mean, he's a scientist," Ronan said. "I'm not sure it's a nine-to-five. And he gives lectures at conferences and universities too."

"Was he giving a lecture around that time?" Nick asked. "Any travel records?"

"Not that we've found," Ronan said. "I'm just saying it's not enough unless Finn says it's him."

They all turned their eyes to Finn. His gaze was focused on the image like he was willing his brain to make a connection. "I just don't know. It makes sense that they'd all look alike, but I didn't expect it to be so hard to I.D. the guy."

"You only saw him for a minute," Elise said softly.

Finn sighed and nodded. "That's true, but his face is seared into my mind. So why can't I make a definite connection to one of these guys?"

"I hate to say it, but it might not be any of them," Nick said. "Facial recognition isn't foolproof on a planet with seven billion people, some of whom aren't in the database at all."

"Great," Finn said. "So you're saying this was all for nothing?"

"Not at all. I'm just saying this process is usually a slow one. It's trying to complete a puzzle with missing pieces and no idea what the end product is supposed to look like."

"So what do you do when you can't find a piece?" Finn asked. "Or when you're not sure one fits?"

"We try it," Ronan said. "We keep trying pieces until you find the one that fits."

"Right now we have three pieces," Finn said. "How do we try them all?"

"That's up to you," Ronan said.

"What are my options?" Finn asked.

"We could contract a photographer to get better pictures." Nick hesitated. "Or you could let go of the whole thing, if you can."

Elise was still getting to know Finn, still learning how to read his moods and expressions, but she knew from the set of his jaw that letting it go wasn't an option. Not yet anyway.

"Or we run these guys down in person," Declan suggested. "Give you a look up close and personal."

Ronan glared at him. Ronan had been Elise's brother-in-law for two years. She knew his expressions by now, knew he was annoyed at Declan for mentioning an option none of them wanted Declan to choose.

Declan shrugged. "What? It's what I'd do."

"Of course it is," Nick grumbled.

"I can go alone," Finn announced, obviously reading the room. "Just give me the information — names, addresses — and I'll be on my way."

Elise held her breath.

"Jesus fuck," Ronan said, shaking his head. "You're not going alone. If you insist on going at all — and I want it on record that I don't advise it — we wouldn't let you do it alone."

"Your advice is noted." Finn stood. "When do we leave?"

11

Finn mulled over the new information all the way home from MIS, his mind on the three men who might have killed Fedir and Iryna, his eyes on Elise's taillights in front of him.

Going to England was a fool's errand. Even he knew that. Statistically, it was more likely the man he was looking for hadn't come up at all during the facial recognition search.

Nick's words echoed in his mind: seven billion people. What were the odds one of the three they'd identified was the man Finn had seen leaving Fedir and Iryna's house while Finn was crouching in the woods with Petro?

Slim to none. End of story.

Except he wasn't ready to let it go. Not if there

was even a chance of finding the man he'd seen. Nothing would bring back Petro's parents, but the little boy deserved justice.

And there was something else: Finn needed to know he hadn't failed them. He couldn't help thinking there were things he hadn't seen while he'd been there, things he hadn't noticed that might have warned him Fedir and Iryna were in danger.

Elise's turn signal blinked in front of him and Finn realized they'd arrived in front of the house. She parked on the street, and he drove past her, looking for another spot close to the house.

Babies had a lot of stuff, and John Thomas was pushing the limit of the word "baby," which meant the little guy was actually kind of heavy after awhile.

He slid into a spot not far from the gate leading to the courtyard and got out of the car. The passing of Thanksgiving had signaled the shift to Christmas and Hanukkah, and the street was festive, with lights strung on the surrounding houses, casting jeweled reflections against the cold pavement.

It had been years since he'd been home for Christmas. While he'd been traveling, he'd been happy to give up the commercialism of the holidays in the West, but now he felt the excitement of anticipation. The holidays had been his favorite time of year as a kid, back when his mom had hung garlands and lights from the walls and banisters in the old house where they'd grown up, the rooms brimming with delicious smells from the kitchen.

Erin had been alive, and they'd gone to see Santa at the mall to tell him what they wanted for Christmas. They'd slid across the house's wood floors in their socks, piling onto the sofa in pajamas like a litter of puppies.

He'd felt safe, like he belonged.

But now when he thought of Christmas, it wasn't his siblings that popped into his mind.

It was her. Elise.

He wanted to walk outside and look at the lights with her gloved hand in his, wanted to watch her cheeks turn pink from the cold, wanted to see what she looked like, sleepy and tousled on Christmas morning.

His brain screamed a warning his heart didn't want to hear. He couldn't get involved with Elise. He wasn't staying in Boston, and the last thing she needed was more grief.

He exited the car and started for the house, expecting Elise to have beaten him there, but when he passed the Audi Julia normally drove, he saw that Elise was still behind the wheel.

He tapped on the window and she turned to look at him. He pointed to the car door and she nodded.

He opened the door and slid into the passenger seat. The engine was off, the air in the car already cooling.

"You okay?" he asked her.

She made no move to answer, just stared out the windshield like there was something more to see than pavement and houses strung with lights.

He was about to repeat the question when she spoke.

"Something has to change."

"What has to change?" he asked.

She turned to look at him, and he was struck again by her beauty. There was something regal about her features, even in shadow.

"I don't know. Just... something," she said. "Have you ever felt that way?"

He thought about the way he'd felt after Erin's overdose: trapped by the sameness of his life, by his family and their expectations that he would go to college and join the military like Ronan, or the police force like Nick and their father.

He'd felt trapped by his own skin.

"Yeah," he said. "Before I left."

"Then you understand." She hesitated. "Which is why I'm wondering if I can come with you."

"Come with me where?" He was having a hard time following her train of thought.

"To London. To Wales. To wherever you're going to see about the three men who matched the sketch," she said.

He didn't know what he'd expected her to say, but it wasn't that. He didn't even know what he would do on the trip — his brothers were the experts. He assumed he would only be there to identify — or not — one of the men as a match to the one who'd been in Fedir and Iryna's house when they'd been killed.

It was even harder to imagine what Elise would do on the trip, not to mention the reaction from Ronan, who Finn already knew would not be on board with the idea.

So why did it appeal to Finn? Why did the thought of leaving the country with Elise, of being close to her 24/7, feel like a good idea when his mind told him it was the furthest thing from it?

"Wouldn't you be bored?" he asked.

"I'm already bored. And I just… I need to get away from here. I feel like everything's gotten so…

narrow." She looked at him. "You know what I mean?"

He nodded. He knew all too well.

"I've never done anything like this before. I don't know how it works," he said.

"Would you mind though?" she asked. "If I came along? I don't want to distract from the point of the trip, but I promise I'll stay out of the way."

I want you to come. I want to be close to you. I want to know you.

"I wouldn't mind. Ronan, on the other hand…"

"Would you vouch for me with him?" she asked. "Tell him I wouldn't be in the way?"

"I don't know if it'll help, but I can put in a word."

She exhaled. "Cool."

"What about work?" he asked. "And finals?"

She stiffened at his mention of work. "I need to get away from those things too."

He nodded. She was a grown woman. She could handle her business.

"What about Julia? How will she feel about you going?" he asked.

She scowled. "I can handle Julia."

12

"I just don't understand." Julia put John Thomas on the floor and sat on Elise's bed. "Help me understand, El."

John Thomas set his block organizer on the floor and dumped out the blocks.

Elise sighed and walked back to her dresser, staring at her sweaters and trying to decide which to take to England. She knew it would be cold, but she had no idea what they'd be doing once they were there.

Convincing Ronan to let her go had been hard enough. She hadn't wanted to push her luck by asking too many questions.

"I have to get away from here, Jules. I'm going nuts. You have Ronan and John Thomas and the work you do for MIS. I have... nothing." Elise chose a red cashmere sweater from the drawer and stuffed it into the small suitcase on the bed.

"That's not true," Julia said. "You have school and the store. You have us."

Elise looked at her and sighed. "I know I have you and Ronan and the rest of the family, and I really do appreciate that, but it's not mine. Like everything I have — the car I drive and the house I live in — they're technically your family."

"But what's — "

"What's mine is yours," Elise finished. "I know, and that's sweet. But at some point I want something of my own, and I'm starting to wonder if I can find that here."

Julia flinched and Elise sat next to her on the bed and took her hand. "You've been amazing. You literally saved my life, and then taking me in here when you were just starting out with Ronan and having JT... that was big, and it made all the difference for me. You gave me a safe place to land, to recover, but I can't stay in a bubble forever. I have to figure out what I want my life — my real life — to look like."

"And I get that," Julia said. "But why now? Why this? What can you do on an MIS trip that will help you figure that out?"

"Probably nothing," Elise said. "But at least it'll give me some mental space to start thinking about it."

"Mama! Mama!" John Thomas held up the block sorter, showing Julia that he'd gotten all the blocks inside.

Elise stood and resumed packing, considering the jeans in her drawer before choosing slim-fitting black ones that would be versatile enough for both casual and dressier occasions. Not that she planned to dress up for anything. This was a work trip for Ronan and Declan, and Finn would be busy with them.

Her stomach fluttered, something she tried to convince herself was nerves and not butterflies at the thought of Finn.

Julia beamed at John Thomas. "Wow! That's amazing, JT. Good job!"

He giggled and dumped out the blocks onto the floor to start over.

Julia turned her attention back to Elise. "If you need some space, wouldn't it be better to... I don't know, take a trip alone or something? Go lay on a beach somewhere with a fruity cocktail in your hand? I've been on work trips with the guys. They're not exactly therapeutic."

Elise avoided Julia's eyes as she tucked the jeans into her bag. "I don't want to go anywhere alone."

Julia grabbed her hand. "Of course you don't. I'm sorry." She hesitated. "We could go — you and me. It would be fun! A sister's trip. I could get Alexa and Nick to watch John Thomas. Or Mom."

"You'd leave JT with Mom?" Elise shook her head. "No. I think this will be perfect. The guys'll be around enough to make me feel safe, but they'll be busy with Finn's case. I can sleep in and take walks, see something new while I get my head together."

John Thomas got to his feet and toddled over to Julia, draping himself across her lap. She ran her fingers through his dark wavy hair. "You tired, buddy?"

"No!" He straightened and ran away from her like a drunken sailor.

Julia laughed and looked at Elise. "Speaking of Mom... are you going to tell her you're leaving?"

They both had a complicated relationship with their mother, who hadn't been very reliable when they'd been growing up. But Julia had always been harder on her than Elise, probably because as the older sister Julia had had to pick up the slack a lot more when they were kids.

"I'll call her. I don't have time to make the trip

before we leave tomorrow. I still have to go into the store and talk to Aliyah and our new boss."

"The creeper?"

Elise had told Julia about her interaction with William Pearson.

"Maybe he's not a creeper," Elise said. "Maybe it was my imagination. I'm probably not the most objective when it comes to that kind of thing."

"If you feel like he's a creeper, he's a creeper. Trust your gut," Julia said.

"I trusted my gut with Seth McFarland, remember? Not a single alarm bell." It was one of the hardest things about recovering from what had happened to her: she couldn't trust herself anymore, couldn't trust her judgement.

About anything.

Seth MacFarland had been a sociopath, and Elise hadn't even caught a hint of it. He'd pushed all the right buttons, something she'd only learned in the aftermath, in therapy, and all she'd seen was a good-looking, sophisticated, successful man who showered her with gifts and made her feel beautiful.

"That was then," Julia said. "You've changed. You've grown. You can trust your instincts, El. I do."

Elise looked at her. "You do?"

"Do you think I'd pawn JT off on you so often if I didn't?" Julia asked.

Elise laughed. "Wow, what a ringing endorsement."

Julia shrugged. "It's true. You know I wouldn't leave him with you if I didn't trust your judgement."

"Trusting me with someone else is one thing. It's myself I have to worry about," Elise said.

Julia stood and leaned in to hug her. "I trust you with you. If this is what you feel you need, I support you."

"Thanks, Jules." Elise walked over to the closet. "Do you think Ronan is super annoyed?"

"He's definitely super annoyed," Julia said. "But he'll get over it. Just stay out of the way. Once he sees that you're not there to be a distraction, he'll be fine. He loves you. He wants to support you too."

Elise knew it was true. It was the only reason Ronan had finally given in to her pleas to be allowed on the trip, even when she could see in his eyes that he still wasn't sold on the idea — that and the fact that Nick and Finn had vouched for her, something she could only assume had happened because she knew they didn't do anything with the business unless it was unanimous, even if grudgingly so.

"I will be quiet as a mouse," Elise said. "I just

want to eat fish and chips and walk along the Thames and sit in old churches."

"I think you're right," Julia said. "I think this will be good for you."

Elise smiled. "Thanks. Me too."

A shadow crossed Julia's features. Elise knew the expression well. It was the one Julia wore when she wanted to say something she knew Elise wouldn't like.

"Just say it," Elise said.

"What?"

"Don't act innocent. I know you too well. Just tell me what's on your mind."

Julia sighed. "Fine. I'm just wondering about Finn."

"What about Finn?" Elise asked.

"You guys seem to have gotten friendly. Is this about him?" Julia asked.

Before her kidnapping, Elise would have lied. Back then she'd seen Julia as judgy rather than concerned, and she hadn't given a second thought to lying to avoid a difficult conversation with her sister.

But that was before Julia had risked everything — had risked her life — to save Elise from Manifest. Julia never had to prove how much she cared about Elise again.

"It's not not about Finn," Elise said.

"What's that supposed to mean?" Julia asked.

Elise sat on the bed and picked at a loose thread in the comforter. "Nothing's happened between us or anything."

"But?"

"It feels like it could? Like it might?"

"Do you think that's a good idea?" Julia asked.

"I don't know," Elise said. "But I'm guessing you don't."

Julia hesitated, and Elise knew she was considering her words. "I just don't want you to get hurt. You've been alone for a while now. I'm guessing it'll be a big deal to open up to someone again, and Finn is... well, he's Finn. I love him, but he literally walked away from his family for eight years. Who knows how long it would have taken him to come home if the thing in Ukraine hadn't happened?"

"I know all that," Elise said. In fact, she'd bet she knew Finn better than Julia at this point. She was under no illusion about the fact that Finn wouldn't stick around once MIS found the answers he needed.

"Hey," Julia said. Elise looked at her. "I'm on your side, El. Really. I just worry about you that's all."

"Well, don't okay? Seriously. I needed you to take

care of me for a while there, but I'm an adult, a grown woman. I can make decisions for myself."

Julia nodded. "Okay."

In spite of the words, Elise could see that Julia was still concerned. Her sister's worry watered the seed of her own: that she was already falling for Finn Murphy, that it was too late to stop it, and that when it was all over, she'd be holding her broken heart in her hands.

She could only hope she'd have the strength to fix it.

13

Finn sat back in the plush leather seats of the plane and took a drink of his whiskey. It had been served in a cut crystal glass by a quiet, efficient flight attendant who looked perfectly at home in the luxe environment of the private jet.

Behind him, Elise was curled up on one of the seats, her long hair pulled back into a ponytail, gaze fixed on the clouds outside the window. Across the aisle from her, Declan dozed, his sunglasses covering his eyes.

Finn took it all in again — the plush seats and wool carpet, the homey lighting that made the place look like a cozy apartment instead of a tin can, the open door that offered a glimpse of the bedroom at the back of the plane.

"This is really yours?" he asked Ronan, sitting across from him, his long legs stretched out between them.

Ronan looked up from his iPad. "It belongs to MIS."

Finn smirked. "Right, but MIS is you, right?"

"MIS is us," Ronan corrected. "Yes."

"Wow. Did you ever think you'd own a private jet?" Finn asked.

Ronan set the iPad aside and looked at him. "No, but it's a matter of convenience, not fun. Not now anyway."

"What do you mean now?" Finn asked.

"Before Kate came back Dec was known to commandeer the jet for the occasional weekend tryst," Ronan said.

"Ah." Since coming home, Finn had gotten the dirt on Declan's pre-Kate-reunion exploits, which had apparently included a lot of bar fights and a string of hookups that had only come to an end after Julia and Ronan had John Thomas. "You don't use it for vacations or anything?"

Ronan took a drink of the beer in his hand. "It's been awhile since I've had a vacation."

"Maybe you should fix that," Finn said. "Travel is good for the soul."

"We did a lot of traveling when we were trying to find Elise. I think we were all happy to be home for a while." Ronan turned the beer bottle in his hand. "Speaking of Elise…"

Finn looked at him. "I figured this was coming."

"There wasn't time before we left Boston," Ronan said. "But I have to ask."

"Whatever it is, I'm almost positive it's none of your business," Finn said. "But ask away."

Anger flashed in Ronan's eyes. "It is my business. Elise is my wife's sister, and you have no idea what she's been through."

"I have an idea," Finn said slowly.

Ronan took another swig of his beer. Finn could tell he was trying to stay calm and not let his temper get away from him by the way he didn't answer right away. Ronan always had an answer for everything. If he was quiet, it was because he was choosing to be quiet, either because he was playing his cards close to the vest or because he was trying to keep his cool.

"Are you sure it's a good idea?" he finally asked. "To start something with Elise?"

"I haven't started anything more than a friendship at this point," Finn said.

"No, but you're thinking about it. You want to."

Finn wouldn't deny it. It would be a lie, and he wasn't a liar. "I'm thinking about it."

"Then my question stands," Ronan said.

It was a question Finn had been asking himself, the sole reason he hadn't already swept Elise into his arms. "I think Elise and I are both adults who can make up our own minds about what's best for us."

"I need you to know how fragile she was when we brought her back, how fragile she still is," Ronan said. "I need you to know how many times Julia ran to her bed when she woke up screaming and crying, how many nights the two of them sat up on the sofa with the TV on because Elise was afraid to sleep."

Finn's heart constricted in his chest at the thought of Elise scared or hurting. "I can't say I'm surprised," he said softly.

Ronan nodded. "So you can see why we're worried."

"We?"

"Julia mentioned it too," Ronan said. "She would have spoken to you herself if she'd had time before we left."

"She's worried about me with Elise?"

"She's worried about anyone with Elise. Julia's worried she's not ready for a relationship, that she's not ready for... intimacy," Ronan said.

Finn squirmed. After eight years on the road, he wasn't used to talking to anyone — let alone his big brother — about his sex life.

Besides, when he thought about Elisa, about getting closer to her, sex wasn't the first thing that came to mind.

Okay, it was there, in the background. He'd be fooling himself if he tried to tell himself otherwise.

But he'd shut down his lust, knowing it was a minefield. What was left was less familiar: a primal desire to protect, to shelter Elise from everything that had ever hurt her, from anything that might hurt her in the future.

"I think that's up to Elise," Finn said.

Ronan shook his head. "Don't be a dick."

"How am I being a dick?"

"Acting like I'm some stranger. I'm your brother. I'm Elise's brother too, for all intents and purposes. I plucked her out of the hands of men who wanted to sell her, Finn. I looked in her eyes and saw nothing but emptiness. I brought her into the house and held my wife while she cried, wondering if her sister would ever be okay again." He shook his head. "Don't fucking act like I'm a stranger."

Finn sighed. "You're right. I'm sorry." Ronan nodded and Finn continued. "I understand why you and Julia are concerned. I'm concerned too. It's why I haven't acted on my feelings yet."

"So you have feelings," Ronan said.

"I wouldn't open up this Pandora's box if I didn't. Sex is easy. If it was only about sex I'd look for something less messy."

"Fuck," Ronan murmured.

"Listen, I'm aware, okay? I know how heavy this all is. I know what's at stake." He glanced back, wanting to make sure Elise couldn't hear them, but she'd tipped her seat back and fallen asleep. He lowered his voice anyway. "I do have feelings for her, which is why I'm being so careful. I would never intentionally hurt her."

"It's not your intentions I'm worried about. Let me ask you this: are you planning to stay after this is all over?"

"In Boston?" Finn asked.

Ronan nodded.

Finn hesitated. "No." It was nice to be back in Boston, to see his family and meet its newest members. But it wasn't home anymore. "I'll be home to visit more often in the future, but I'm not sure I'll ever settle down in one place."

"Does Elise know that? What will it mean for her when you leave?" Ronan asked.

Finn tried to follow the question to its logical conclusion but couldn't. It was too abstract. He didn't even know if Elise had feelings for him. Maybe nothing would develop between them at all. Maybe it would be less thrilling than he imagined.

Fool.

He ignored the voice in his head. "I don't have a crystal ball, Ro. But I'll be careful, okay? I'll be honest with her on the front end about my intentions. I'll make sure it doesn't get out of hand."

Ronan sighed and shook his head. "You're an adult, Finn. I can't tell you what to do. I'm just asking you to consider the situation before you move forward."

"I will," Finn promised.

Ronan turned back to his iPad, and Finn looked out the window, the clouds below them cast gold by the setting sun, which looked almost close enough to touch.

But Ronan's words weren't the ones running on a loop in his mind.

They were his: *I'll make sure it doesn't get out of hand.*

Even now, before anything had happened between him and Elise, he had a feeing he wouldn't have control over what happened between them.

Even now, he knew holding her, touching her, would set off an inferno he wouldn't be able to extinguish.

14

Elise tucked her chin into her scarf and buried her gloved hands deeper into her coat.

"Come to England in December, they said. It'll be fun, they said." She muttered the words, but even now, freezing her ass off at the top of a cliff, the sky steely overhead, she wouldn't change a thing.

She'd gotten used to traversing unfamiliar places alone over the past five days, wiling away her time just like she'd planned — eating and walking and sitting and staring at an ever-unfolding series of breathtaking scenery.

They'd started in Wales, where Finn, Ronan, and Declan had cased the hotel company where Oliver Paine, one of the men who came up in the facial recognition search, worked.

While they waited for him to appear, to get close enough for Finn to get a good look at him, Elise had walked every street of the little fishing village near the house where they'd stayed.

She'd been nervous about being too far from the house at first, the way she'd felt out on her own in Boston when she'd first come back from her ordeal with Manifest. She'd had to make frequent stops, leaning against old brick buildings and sitting on iron benches to catch her breath, walking herself through the breathing exercises she'd been taught by her therapist.

After the first couple of days, she'd started to feel safe, and she'd spent hours staring out at the water, eating her weight in hot fried fish, smiling at passersby, and trying to figure out what they said to her in their unusual accent.

Then Finn was able to get a good look at Oliver Paine during a company lunch. Finn had confirmed that he hadn't been the man in Ukraine, and they'd picked up and gone to Cornwall.

She'd prepared herself for another rough day or two, knowing that unfamiliar places still made her feel unsafe, made her half-expect someone to jump out and shove her in a car like...

No, she wouldn't think about that.

But Cornwall had been a surprise. The house where they were staying (Ronan's? Declan's? It wasn't clear but Elise had the feeling it was owned by one of the brothers) was set up on a cliff, too far from town to walk in the cold.

A set of stairs were cut into the cliff face, leading to a wide beach at the base of the cliffs, the roiling water stretched out as far as the eye could see.

Maybe it was all that space, but Elise had immediately felt at home there. There were no other houses in sight, and no matter where she stood, she could see for miles in almost every direction: no alleys where someone might hide, no cars that might stop suddenly at the curb, just her and the soaring cliffs and the wild sea.

There was no place to buy fish and chips, so she'd taken to packing food from the house, along with a thermos of soup or tea. Then, while Finn, Ronan, and Nick plotted a way into the estate of Ronald Wellick, the commodities trader, she walked and walked.

After a couple of hours, she'd either unfold her blanket at the top of the cliff or she'd traverse the staircase to the beach itself. Other than the occasional photo, she didn't bother removing her phone from her pocket. She just sat and stared at the horizon, letting her mind go blissfully blank.

Sometimes she even fell asleep, waking to find the sun lower on the horizon, her hair tangled from the wind, cheeks numb, salt on her lips.

The sea air and cold was like an anesthetic. Sometimes she could barely make it through dinner without nodding off, the sound of Finn and his brothers talking acting as a kind of lullaby, soothing her to sleep.

She hadn't had to take a single sleeping pill since they'd been in Cornwall.

For the most part, Ronan and Declan had seemed to accept her presence on the trip. She still caught Ronan looking at her and Finn from time to time, usually when the two of them were lost in their own conversation, but he'd stopped being moody and quiet around her when he'd realized she wouldn't interfere in their operation.

She caught movement out of her peripheral vision and pulled her eyes away from the water to see a figure walking toward her in the distance. She knew even without being able to see the person's facial features that it was Finn, knew by the way he ambled toward her, slowly and unselfconsciously, the same way he did everything.

She tried to ignore the way her heart beat faster as he came into the view. Tried to ignore the fluttering in her stomach.

It was an exercise in futility and she knew it, had known it for weeks, but especially since they'd left Boston. When they weren't busy with the case, Finn joined her on her walks, the two of them often walking for an hour or more in silence that somehow wasn't awkward.

When she woke up in the morning, it was Finn who handed her a cup of coffee. One night when she'd fallen asleep over her dinner, she'd woken up to find herself being swept into Finn's arms.

She'd tucked her face against his chest and pretended to stay asleep, wanting to breathe him in, sinking into the solid strength of him and the way he made her feel like nothing in the world could touch her.

They'd been teetering on the line between friendship and romance, maintaining what little balance they had mostly because Ronan and Declan were usually around, a reminder of all that was at stake if they gave into what she was sure was a mutual attraction.

"Hey," he said when he was close enough for her to hear him.

Bundled up in a navy peacoat that brought out the blue in his eyes, his legs clad in well-worn jeans, he looked as good as ever, and she felt the stirring of something long dead between her legs.

"Hey. You done for the day?" She tried to focus on his face, the strong cheekbones and chiseled jaw, the beard that would scratch against the inside of her thighs...

Ooookay. That wasn't helping.

"We're done here period," he said.

"Oh no... it's not him?"

Finn shook his head. "He had a meeting in Truro. We caught him in town."

"I'm sorry." She didn't bother to ask if he was sure. You didn't forget the faces of people who did horrific things to people you cared about, of people who did horrific things to you. She knew that firsthand.

The only reason Finn hadn't been able to identify them via the photographs was because they'd all matched to the same sketch. There were no mannerisms in a photograph, no facial tics or vocal characteristics, nothing to set one apart from the other.

But in person? Finn would know.

He shrugged. "I guess it's on to Aberdeen then."

She nodded, her heart sinking. "I guess so."

She wasn't ready to go home, but Aberdeen was their last stop, the last chance Finn had to match one of the photographs to the man who'd murdered his friends in Ukraine.

He rubbed his hands together. He hadn't worn gloves. "Come on, let's head back. It's freezing."

"When do we leave?" she asked as they started walking.

"In the morning."

She looked out over the water. "I'm going to miss it here."

He looked down at her. "It agrees with you."

"You think?"

He nodded. "You seem happy. You seem... at peace."

"I don't seem that way in Boston?" she asked.

He smiled. "Is this a trick question?"

"Just an honest one," she said.

He looked straight ahead, seeming to consider his words. "Not really, no. Do you feel at peace in Boston?"

"I feel..." She searched for the right word. "Trapped. So I guess that would be a no."

"So not that?"

She looked at him. "What does that mean?"

"People spend a lot of time trying to figure out

what they want, but sometimes it's enough to know what you don't want. You know? As in, I don't know what I want, but I know it's not this."

"Not this," she murmured.

"Exactly. Maybe getting away made it easier to see that even though you don't know what you do want, you do know it's not what you have now," he said.

"Maybe."

It made sense. That feeling of being unsettled, of being ill at ease even when she was at home or the store.

"You'll figure it out. Everything will happen in its own time," he said.

He took her hand as they continued walking and she forced herself not to look at him. Her feelings were becoming impossible to deny. She feared they would be written all over her face, that she wouldn't be able to hide them, that the last crumbling remnants of the wall she'd erected between them would fall.

She wasn't imagining the tension between them. It was there, as thick as the morning fog in Cornwall, which blocked out the edge of the cliff and even the sea itself. It would fall away once one or the other of them stepped into it. After that, there would be no going back.

She took a breath of cold, salty air and let the thoughts fall away.

Everything will happen in its own time.

She suddenly believed it, and she let herself savor the moment, the feel of his big hand through the fabric of her gloves, the refuge of his broad shoulders blocking the worst of the wind rolling in off the sea.

But in the back of her mind, she knew the reprieve was temporary. "Not this" sounded like enough in a hypothetical situation, but in her real life she would have to do the work of actually choosing something.

And right now, the only thing she was absolutely sure she wanted was him.

15

Finn looked up from his coffee and toast when Elise entered the kitchen. "Morning," he said.

"Good morning." She yawned and went to the cupboard to get a mug, then made a cup of coffee with the machine on the counter.

They'd been in Scotland for only two days, and none of them were any closer to becoming morning tea converts than they'd been when they'd arrived in Wales ten days earlier.

He'd stopped being surprised by the fact that his brothers seemed to own property all over England. The flat in Aberdeen was housed in a quaint old building, but inside it was as well-appointed as the houses they'd stayed in while in Wales and Cornwall, complete with big windows, four bedrooms, and a gourmet kitchen open to a large living area.

Elise sat at the farm table in the kitchen table and took a sip of the coffee. He tried not to stare, but it wasn't easy, even with all the practice he'd gotten lately. She was wearing flannel pajama bottoms and a long-sleeved T-shirt, plus an oversized cardigan she'd bought in Wales. Her hair was piled on top of her head in a mess of waves, some of which escaped to frame her face.

"Where is everyone?" she asked.

"Turns out Isaac Fleming is out of town," Finn said, taking a bite of toast. He was glad he had something to do with his hands, something besides reaching out and tucking the loose strand of hair behind her ear.

Something besides leaning in to kiss her.

"Oh, no... really?" she said.

He nodded.

"Any idea when he'll be back?" she asked.

He shook his head. "We can't even find a record of him on a flight. Clay's working on the charter flight plans out of Heathrow."

"How do you know he's out of town then?"

"Dec and I were staking out his house early this morning. We saw him leave and tailed him to the charter terminal at the airport, but I didn't get a good look at him before he got in the car."

"Damn," she said.

"Yeah," Finn agreed.

"So what's the plan?" she asked.

"Dec's sleeping off his stakeout. Ronan's out buying gifts for Julia and JT until we hear back from Clay. Hopefully we'll know more tonight."

"What about you?" she asked. "What are you going to do while you wait?"

He took a drink of coffee. This was it. His last chance to back out.

"Actually, I was thinking I'd hang with you today. If that's all right, I mean."

Her cheeks turned pink. "Absolutely, but I was just planning to walk today, maybe see some of the old churches." Her gaze strayed to the window, the perpetually gray sky visible from the flat's gourmet kitchen. "It's not great walking weather, I guess."

He grinned. "Are you saying I can't handle it?"

She laughed. "I know you're an all-weather guy, I just didn't want you to feel obligated if it's not your idea of a good time."

"And I don't want you to feel obligated if you'd rather spend the day alone," he said.

She smiled and shook her head. "If we keep

being polite we'll still be sitting here at dinner." She stood. "I'm going to get ready. You're welcome to come if you want."

"Then I'll come," he said. "I'll just secretly wonder if you really want me along."

She met his eyes and he felt like he was being pulled into their orbit. He had to fight the urge to step toward her.

"I want you along," she said.

He held her gaze and thought he could almost hear the energy crackling between them. "Good."

He watched her leave the room, forcing himself not to look at her ass, lithe but shapely under the soft flannel of her pajama pants.

Jesus. He needed to get himself under control, needed to move slowly with Elise, not freak her out.

It sounded easy enough, but he suddenly had the feeling it was going to be the hardest thing he'd ever done.

They spent the morning walking Aberdeen, turning off the busy commercial streets and exploring the narrow cobblestone lanes that crisscrossed the city. He'd expected Elise to have a guidebook, some kind of plan for the sights she wanted to see, but it quickly became apparent that she was just wandering.

It was exactly the way he liked to travel — no book, no itinerary, no schedule. Just him and a strange city or town and the time and freedom to go where his feet took him.

She was quiet as they walked, yet another thing he liked about her: she never felt the need to fill their silences with chatter. It was almost like traveling alone until he looked down and saw her walking next to him.

He'd wondered if it might feel uncomfortably intimate after traveling alone for all of his adult life, but walking with her in Scotland was no different than being with her anywhere else. The sight of her face looking up at him sent a rush of warmth into his chest, a surge of happiness through his body.

He was happy to be with her, a feeling that was foreign to him.

The city was decked out for the coming holidays, its lampposts decorated with wreaths, lights strung across the streets like jeweled banners. Elaborately decorated Christmas trees popped up on almost every street, and everywhere he looked, people rushed around, clutching shopping bags, entering and exiting the boutiques nestled among historic buildings. It was the most festive he'd felt around Christmas since he'd left Boston and the painful memories of their once-happy family holidays.

He and Elise stopped to look up at the buildings, many of them hundreds of years old, craning their necks to take in old stone, elaborate ironwork, and Gothic windows. They stopped at the Tollbooth museum for a look at a 17th-century jail, complete with a guillotine, but other than that, they remained outside, chins tucked into their scarves and hands ensconced in gloves.

They wandered the streets of Old Aberdeen, an area that was once separate from the rest of the city, and stopped for lunch at a tiny pub where they warmed their hands around cups of hot tea and their stomachs with thick, crusty bread and bowls of cullen skink, a creamy fish stew.

Over lunch, Elise told him more about her childhood, elaborating on the few details he'd heard from Nick. Listening to her talk about her mom — largely drunk, absent, or wrapped up in a new man — he'd begun to see where she'd gotten the strength that had helped her survive when Manifest kidnapped her.

She looked back on the years of her childhood

with a mixture of philosophical sorrow and acceptance, crediting Julia and her grandfather, the man who'd initially hired Ronan to find her, with helping her through it.

She seemed at peace with it all, even with her mom, although Finn knew from talking to Ronan that forgiveness had been harder for Julia to come by.

Elise asked him about growing up in the Murphy house, gently probing the death of his mother and Erin's overdose. There was no pity in her eyes when he told her how it had been, about his mom dying in the bedroom upstairs, his father turning gray and small, the Murphy kids skulking quietly around the house, waiting for her to die, desperate for her not to die. About Erin's headlong rush into heroin addiction, something that seemed to take forever and no time at all, about her death and the way the beating heart of the family had seemed to stop after that.

It was a heavy conversation, one he'd never had with anyone. There had been women over the years — he wasn't a monk — but they'd been relationships of convenience in one way or another: women traveling in his direction, working on one of the farms or in one of the pubs where he earned money along the way, staying in his hostel or campsite, their guaranteed parting always a bit of a relief.

Now he felt his connection to Elise growing deeper and more complex. It both thrilled and scared him — not for himself, but for Elise, because there was no doubt in his mind that once he figured out what had happened to Fedir and Iryna, he would be back on the road with nothing but his pack on his back.

I feel like I need to tell you how fragile she was when we brought her back, how fragile she still is...

Ronan's words echoed in his mind as they finished lunch and headed back outside.

Neither of them were anxious to be cold again after the cozy warmth of the pub, so they broke down and hired a car to take them to Torry Battery, the remnants of an old artillery fort that had been built to defend the harbor from Napoleon the Third.

The battery was right on the water, the air cold enough to make Finn suck in his breath as they exited the hired car. The city was visible across an inlet on one side of the peninsula, the sea stretching gray and rough toward the horizon on the other.

"Wow," Elise said, tightening her scarf around her chin. "It's freezing."

He smiled above his own scarf. "Change your mind?"

Her hazel eyes flashed. "No way. I didn't come all the way to Scotland to sit in the flat. Let's go."

"That's the spirit."

Not much remained of the battery. They walked through a brick archway and along the brick walls, then explored what was left of the rooms that had once been used to mount guns and watch for invaders.

Not ready to leave, they headed toward a lighthouse in the distance. The wind roared in off the sea, and they walked silently side by side as they both looked out over the water.

Elise was shivering by the time they reached the lighthouse. It was deserted: no one but them had been crazy enough to make the walk in such rough weather.

Finn pulled her toward the side of the building. "Here, come in out of the wind."

He leaned against the lighthouse, her hand still in his. Then she was staring up into his eyes, breathless, lips parted.

She reached up to touch his face. "Finn..."

He spun her around so that her back was against

the lighthouse, his body sheltering her from the wind and cold.

Taking her face in his hands, he let his gaze roam her eyes and cheeks and mouth, drinking her in the way he'd always wanted to, the way he'd only dared in stolen glances when he'd thought no one was watching.

Now she was right here in his arms, her body warm against his through the bulk of their coats. It was like a dream — a dream he never wanted to end, but one that would end just the same. The only question was how badly they'd both be hurt when it was all over.

16

Elise had known it, hadn't she? Had known when Finn asked to come with her that today would be the day the final barrier fell between them? There was an inevitability to it, the feeling that they'd been careening to this end all along, that deep down they'd both known it.

She slid her arms around his waist and looked up at him, lost in the blue of his eyes, an ocean of calm amid the stormy sea around her. She knew what he was going to say next, had known what he was going to say since she'd first felt their friendship blossom into something more.

He rubbed the pad of his thumb against her full lips and stroked her cheek. She could feel the heat of his breath on her mouth. "If we do this, there's no going back. And Elise... I can't promise you anything. I can't promise you tomorrow."

She pulled him more tightly against her, feeling the length of his denim-clad thighs pressed against hers, like a lightning rod in a storm.

She'd spent the last few weeks thinking about all the ways it could go wrong, all the ways she could be hurt. It hadn't changed anything. She was willing to risk pain for a chance to feel joy again.

"I don't want to go back," she said. "I just want you right now. I want this."

He rubbed his cheek against hers. The friction of his beard sent a bolt of desire to her core.

"Elise, Elise, Elise..." He murmured the words like a prayer, dropping tender kisses along her cheekbone and jaw. "You don't know how badly I've wanted you."

A shiver ran up her spine when his tongue, hot and wet, flicked out to taste the sensitive skin behind her ear. Her nipples hardened under her sweater, every nerve in her body on fire as he kissed his way back to her mouth.

He touched his lips to the corners of her mouth in a duet of reverent kisses, then lingered there, his breath hot in the moment before he lowered his head.

The kiss was gentle at first, almost chaste. It had been so long since she'd been intimate with a man. She hadn't known how it would feel, hadn't known if she would be able to tolerate it when the moment finally came.

Now she sighed against his lips, sinking into their softness, leaning into his body and wrapping her arms more tightly around him.

He groaned, taking possession of her mouth, his tongue sliding languidly between her lips.

A frenzy of hunger unfolded at her center. It took her breath away, and she pressed against him, feeling the length of his erection through his jeans, evidence of how much he wanted her.

It was something she'd wondered: if anyone would ever want her again, if anyone would ever be able to look at her with desire, knowing what had happened to her.

But there was no doubt in his kiss, in the urgent stroke of his tongue sweeping her mouth. She met it with her own, the hot need of it stoking her passion, turning the sparks in her belly into a fire she didn't want to control.

He slanted his mouth over hers, taking the kiss deeper, and what was left of the ground underneath her fell away. His hands slid down her neck, pushing her scarf aside to stroke the hollow at the base of her throat with his thumb.

The cold had disappeared. The sensation of his touch at such a tender intersection of her body, so close to her full and aching breasts, only made her want more. She wanted to tear off his jacket, pull off their clothes, feel the slide of his bare skin against her own.

The kiss was kerosene on the embers of her body, embers she'd thought were dead and cold, nothing but black ash. It breathed life into all the empty corners of her body, all the places that had felt lost to her forever.

He pulled away, breathing hard, his eyes like molten sapphire. They burned into hers as he touched her forehead with his own. "I don't want to hurt you."

She shook her head. "No. Don't do that, Finn. Don't you dare try to protect me. I can take care of myself, make my own decisions. I need…" She trailed off, looking for the right words.

"What do you need, El?" His voice was soft. It was the first time he'd used the nickname. "Tell me."

"I need to be able to trust that you don't feel sorry for me. That everything you do and everything you say is real, that you're not doing it or saying it because you're trying to protect me," she said.

"I will protect you." The ferocity in his voice took her by surprise.

"That's not what I want." She reached up to touch his face. "I've been protected long enough. If we're going to be together, I want it to be real. Pain and all. You have to promise me."

His eyes darkened. He didn't say anything for so long, she wondered if he'd changed his mind.

"I promise," he finally said.

She kissed him. "Good."

He pulled her closer and she buried her face in his jacket. She tried to tell herself the thumping of her heart was excitement, passion. But deep down she knew it for the fear it was. Whatever happened now, whatever pain came when he left — and he would leave — she had no one to blame but herself.

17

"Fuck me, it's cold." Declan's voice sounded in Finn's ear piece. Finn could almost hear Dec rubbing his hands together over the comms system.

"Any sign of him?" Finn surveyed the busy Aberdeen street. It was nearly lunchtime on a Wednesday, and pedestrians hurried to and fro, chins tucked into scarves, gloved hands clutching handbags and packages. The sky was a clear pale blue, the sun bright overhead but doing little to warm the air.

"Not yet," Declan said.

"Ro?" Finn asked.

"You'll know if I see something." Ronan's voice was bored through the headset. Finn didn't know a lot about MIS' previous jobs, but he imagined stalking a professor through city streets during the day was on the low end of the excitement curve.

Finn leaned back against the brick facade of the building that had been his stakeout point for the past hour. Isaac Fleming had arrived back in town the night before, something they only knew because of the security camera they'd hidden in the street lamp outside his gated property.

He'd been gone three days, long enough for Clay to trace his charter jet's flight plan to a town in Poland. There hadn't been time to dig for more details. Instead Finn, Ronan, and Declan had watched Fleming exit a black SUV in front of his house outside of the city.

They'd spent the night reviewing the video feed from the security camera, hoping to get a clear enough look that Finn would be able to ID the guy — or not.

But it had been impossible. The angle of the camera was all wrong, the man turning too quickly for the gate that protected his house in the country. They'd frozen the image just before his turn, had expanded it, played with the contrast, everything they could think of to give Finn a clearer look.

It hadn't helped. Finn thought there was something familiar in the angle of the man's chin, his gait as he strode toward the gate's control panel, but he couldn't be sure. Was he seeing the sketch that was seared into his mind? Projecting mannerisms onto the man out of desperation?

They'd given up in the wee hours of the morning, deciding instead to tail Fleming to his lab the next day. Thanks to the recon that had been done before they got to Scotland (by Clay? By someone else? Finn added it to the list of things he didn't know about his brothers' business), they knew he left the lab for lunch at 12:30 p.m., knew he walked to a local cafe where he ordered something different every day, knew he ate on a bench in Johnston Gardens in all but the most inclement of weather.

Finn checked his phone. 12:25 p.m.

He sighed and stuffed his hands into his pockets, watching his breath fog the air as it left his body.

His thoughts turned to Elise, which was no surprise. When his mind hadn't been on Isaac Fleming, it had been on her, on the way it had felt to finally hold her in his arms, to kiss her, to know he hadn't been imagining their attraction.

They'd stood outside the lighthouse until their faces were numb. Finn hadn't wanted to break the spell, hadn't wanted to return to the real world where he would have to deal with Ronan's disapproval and the unfinished business of Fedir and Iryna's murder.

On the other hand, it had been for the best. Crossing the line of their friendship felt like a dam breaking, and even though she'd asked him not to worry about her, not to try and protect her, he wasn't sure it was a promise he could keep.

He did worry. He did want to protect her.

He just wasn't sure he could protect her from himself.

"Heads up," Ronan's voice sounded in Finn's ear. "Fleming is on the move and headed your way, Dec."

Finn straightened. Declan was positioned halfway between the lab and the cafe where Fleming picked up his lunch. It was his job to make sure Fleming didn't make a detour between the two locations.

Finn would pick up Fleming at the cafe and keep eyes on him until he could either positively ID the guy or rule him out once and for all. If that meant tailing him through Johnston Gardens, so be it.

"I'm on it," Dec said. Then, a couple minutes later. "I'm on his tail now. Looks like he's heading for the cafe. Still wearing the gray coat."

Finn looked around at the sea of pedestrians in black, gray, and navy coats.

Great.

He pulled out his phone and held it to his ear, trying to affect an expression of concentration while he kept his eyes on the sidewalk, watching for Isaac Fleming in the crowd.

"We're a block from you," Dec said in his ear.

Adrenaline coursed through Finn's veins. After weeks of trying to find the man who'd been party to Fedir and Iryna's murder, Finn would either find him today or be forced to call quits on the search.

He suddenly didn't know which way he wanted it to go.

"I think I see him," Finn said, his gaze snagging on a slender figure wearing a gray coat and walking briskly toward the cafe.

Isaac Fleming was looking down at his phone, his face in shadow. Declan came into view behind him, towering over the crowd.

"Can you see his face?" Ronan asked.

"He's looking at his phone," Finn said.

"Fuck," Ronan muttered.

Fleming was closing the distance between them, his face still bowed to his phone. As he approached, Finn studied what he could see of the man's face. He hadn't imagined it in the security cam footage: there was something about the man's chin, about the set of his shoulders.

He was almost holding his breath by the time Fleming reached the door of the cafe.

Finn wasn't thinking when he stepped out in front of him and reached for the door.

He just had to know.

"Jesus fuck," he heard Declan curse into the earpiece. "We told you not to draw attention to yourself."

They had told him that, but right then, it didn't matter. This was Finn's chance, and he wasn't going to blow it.

He pulled open the door for Fleming, forced himself to smile when the man looked at him.

It was like a punch to the gut: the widow's peak and slightly pointed chin, the empty brown eyes Finn saw in his nightmares.

Because this man was cruel. Finn knew that even though he didn't know him.

Fleming had been in Ukraine, and while Finn had no way of knowing if he was the one who'd pulled the trigger and killed Fedir and Iryna, he'd undoubtedly been in the room.

"Thank you," the man said in a brisk accent that Finn now realized wasn't British at all, but Scottish.

Finn forced himself to nod, then let the door shut behind the man as he sunk back against the building's facade.

"We told you not to let him see you," Declan said, scowling.

"It's him," Finn said. "Isaac Fleming is the man who was in the room with the mercenaries who killed Petro's parents."

"Are you sure?"

Finn reached for the door of the cafe without thinking.

Declan's hand clamped down on his arm. "What are you doing?"

"I'm going after him."

Declan blocked his way. "No, you're not."

Finn tried to shoulder past him. "Fuck you, I'm not."

Declan slammed him back against the brick building. It took him by surprise. There was a time when getting pushed around by his brothers had been a daily occurrence.

That time had long since passed.

"This isn't how we do things," Declan said.

"I don't care," Finn gritted out.

Declan didn't let up the pressure on Finn's chest. "Do you want him to really pay? For watching them die?"

Finn was breathing hard even though he'd hardly moved. He nodded.

"Then trust me." Declan let Finn go. "Let's get out of here."

18

Elise tucked her arm in Finn's and sighed as they left the flat's lobby and headed out into the street. It was a relief to be outside, to feel the sting of cold on her cheeks and the expanse of space around them.

It had been three days since they'd admitted their feelings to each other. Since then, they'd been walking on eggshells around Ronan and Declan, first because they weren't sure how open to be about what was happening between them, and then because Finn had identified Isaac Fleming as the man who'd been present when his friends were murdered in Ukraine.

It was a stew of tension and stress, Elise and Finn still processing the weight of their confession at the lighthouse while Finn also grappled with what to do about Isaac Fleming.

Elise had tried to give him space to figure it all out. The last thing she wanted was for their relationship — whatever that meant right now — to be a source of added stress. She felt like she'd been waiting her whole life for Finn Murphy. She could wait a few days or weeks for him to sort everything out.

And he did have to sort it out. Ronan and Declan had told Finn they would support him in whatever next steps he wanted to take with Fleming, but Christmas was right around the corner and they were both eager to get back to their families.

"It feels good to be outside," Finn said next to her.

"It does." She hesitated as they waited on a street corner to cross. Festive lights decorated the flats around the neighborhood, candles in the windows, wreaths on the doors. It was a strange contrast to the heavy mood in the flat over the past couple of days. "I've been worried about you."

He looked down at her in surprise. "About me?"

The light changed and they started across the street.

She nodded. "I know it was a shock finding Isaac Fleming, knowing he was the one who..."

She trailed off, not wanting to bring Fedir and Iryna's murder too close.

Finn nodded. "I just don't get it. What would a scientist like Fleming — a *geologist* — be doing in a tiny village in Ukraine? And why would he be part of a murder there?"

Elise had been puzzling over the question too. They all had. "Is it something you want to pursue?"

"I don't know how to pursue it," he said. "No international authority is going to be interested in a months-old murder of two rural villagers in Ukraine, and the local police didn't seem overly interested — or competent — either."

She looked up at him, struck again by how beautiful he was, even in profile. "Isn't that... weird?"

"It's more than weird — it's suspicious," he said. "I thought so when it happened too, but there was so much going on, and there was Petro to think about too. I thought I was misreading the signals, that maybe it was a cultural difference. It's not like the police in America are always compassionate."

"So what are your options?" she asked. "If you want to pursue it, I mean."

She didn't try to fill the silence that spread out

between them. Finn was a thinker. He liked to draw conclusions before talking about them.

"I could beat the shit out of him," Finn said. "Try to get him to confess, to tell me why Fedir and Iryna were killed and who else was involved."

"I sense a 'but.'"

"There's no guarantee he'll come clean, or that he'll even tell the truth. He could deny it or send me on a wild goose chase," Finn said.

"I don't disagree." The thought of Finn beating someone up for information should have bothered her more than it did. Maybe she'd been part of the Murphy house for too long. "And you can't find Fedir and Iryna's killer from jail if Fleming presses charges."

"I could try to find out more, dig into Fleming's contacts and background, try to figure out how he was involved in the murders and why, see if the information leads me to a bigger picture."

Elise chose her words carefully. "What would that change?"

He stared ahead while they walked, his gaze on some distant point down the street. "Nothing. But none of this will change anything. Fedir and Iryna will still be dead, whatever I decide to do." He drew in a breath and it exited his mouth in a puff of smoke from the cold. "Which brings me to the last option."

"Which is?"

"Let it go. Just accept that I'm never going to have all the answers and let it go," he said.

"How do you feel about that?" The question, asked by her therapist a hundred times over the past two years, slipped from her mouth.

"Like shit," he said. "But that doesn't mean it isn't the right answer."

She sighed and leaned her head on his arm, savoring the solidity of it, the wall of his body next to hers. "I'm sorry. I don't know what to say. I don't know what to do."

"I can think of something." He took her hand and pulled her out of the flow of pedestrian traffic, pinning her gently against the stone facade of a quaint restaurant. He looked down at her, dragged his knuckles across her cheek.

She could hardly breathe when he looked at her.

They'd hardly been alone since the day at the lighthouse. Finn had identified Isaac Fleming the next day, and they'd been in the flat ever since, Finn raging abut Fleming, Ronan and Declan pacing, talking in low voices when Finn was out of the room when they thought Elise wasn't paying attention.

They'd stolen time in the kitchen before anyone else was awake, when they passed each other in the hall, in secret glances and hidden touches, neither of them ready to talk about their relationship with Ronan and Declan.

The way he looked at her quickened her pulse. He was wild, dangerous in a way that was different from his brothers, in a way that would challenge all the things she believed about herself and her life.

She slid her arms around his waist and looked up at him. "There are an awful lot of people around, but what do you have in mind?"

He bent his head to kiss her, his lips soft and sure on her own, his breath warm against her face when he pulled away. "Christmas in Scotland."

"Christmas?" It wasn't what she'd expected him to say.

"If you want," he said. "Ronan and Dec will go back to the States. They have families, so I get it. I'm just not ready. Going back feels like I've made up my mind to accept Fedir and Iryna's murder, and I haven't. Not yet anyway. I have to figure out what to do next." He twirled a lock of her hair, loose under a knit cap, around his finger. "I'd rather do it here, with you."

"Christmas in Scotland..." The idea wasn't

entirely crazy. What scared her, what caused a knot of fear to tighten in her stomach, was that she knew what it would mean for her.

Spending Christmas together would solidify her time with Finn into something tangible, a memory that would haunt her every December, through all the long years when he would be absent from her life, when he would have moved on to Africa or Germany or Croatia or Japan.

"I know you'll miss Julia and John Thomas, so if you don't want to, I understand," he said. "No pressure."

She stood on her tiptoes and kissed him. "I'd love to spend Christmas with you."

Her therapist was always encouraging Elise to be mindful, to live in the moment instead of the terrifying past, the uncertain future. Well, this was her, living in the moment with Finn.

For better or worse.

19

"I can't stay," Ronan said. "Not at Christmas."

Declan shook his head. "Me neither."

Finn leaned back into the sofa. He hadn't realized he'd been leaning forward while he told them he was staying in Scotland for Christmas. "I'm not asking you to."

"What about Elise?" Ronan asked.

"She's staying too," Finn said.

She'd been willing to face Ronan and Declan with Finn, to tell them herself that she wanted to stay, but Finn hadn't wanted to expose her to Ronan's disapproval. Finn was confident Ronan would come around, but he'd predicted the reaction he was getting now: Ronan's grimace of disapproval, the tension in his jaw that said he was gearing up for a fight.

Elise could handle Ronan, but Finn had wanted to pave the way, which was how he came to be sitting in the living room of the flat, outlining their plans to stay in Scotland through the New Year. Elise, sensing something was going down, had stepped out to do some Christmas shopping.

Ronan rubbed a hand over the short hair at the top of his head. "Jesus, Finn."

"We've talked about this." Finn wasn't up for another lecture about Elise. "I'm not asking your permission, just letting you know my plans."

"What else?" Ronan asked.

"Nothing else," Finn said.

Declan leaned forward, his eyes piercing. "We need you to be straight with us here. About Fleming."

"I'm not going to fuck with Fleming," Finn said. "Not over the holiday."

"What's that supposed to mean?" Ronan asked.

"It means I don't know yet what I want to do about him long-term. It's part of why I want to stay. I need some time and space to think."

As much as he loved his family, as much as he

sometimes regretted all the birthdays and holidays he'd missed over the years, a noisy Christmas with them wasn't going to help him figure out his next step.

And it wasn't exactly conducive to his relationship with Elise either.

"So we don't have to worry about you ending up in jail?" Ronan asked. "Because that's not something I want on my plate right now."

"You don't have to worry. We're just going to hunker down in the flat, keep the holiday simple," Finn said.

Ronan lifted his eyebrows. "Simple?"

Finn met his gaze. "Yes, simple."

Because while the circumstances surrounding his relationship with Elise weren't simple — the trauma from her past, his own inability to commit to anything or anyone, the entanglement of their families — his feelings were: he wanted to be with her as much as possible while he had the chance, wanted to learn her and know her.

That was all.

Ronan stood and paced to the big window overlooking the street below. "I think you're a fool."

"Noted." Finn looked at Declan. "What about you?"

Declan shrugged. "You're both adults." Ronan

turned to glare at him and Declan continued. "Obviously, I don't want to see Elise hurt — she's part of the family — but it's not my place to interfere."

"Easy for you to say," Ronan muttered.

"I'll call Julia," Finn said. "Try to reassure her."

"Give it your best shot." Ronan didn't sound hopeful.

Finn stood, ready to take the conversation in another direction. "Whatever I decide about Fleming, I don't expect you to be part of it. I appreciate what you've done so far — I couldn't have found him without you — but I know you have families and paying clients. I can take the next steps myself, whatever they end up being."

Ronan slapped him on the back of the head, the way he had when Finn had been little and it had made him feel like his brain was rattling around inside his skull. This time the gesture felt affectionate. "Don't be an idiot. Whatever you decide, you won't be alone."

Finn nodded. "Thanks."

"For what?" Ronan asked.

"For being here."

"We've been here all along," Declan said, rising to his feet.

There was no accusation in the words, but that

didn't stop Finn from feeling guilty. They *had* been there all along — for each other and for him. It had been Finn's choice to walk alone.

He was starting to see that making that choice meant he'd turned his backs on them, even if it hadn't been intentional. He was the one who had made it hard to find him, who'd taken pride in being unreachable, in more ways than one. How many hard times had he missed? How many low points when one of his brothers might have needed him? When they might have turned to him?

He didn't see a world in which he'd want to stay in Boston, where he'd want to put down the kind of roots Ronan, Nick, and Declan had put down, but that didn't mean he had to be alone. It didn't mean he had to turn his back on them.

"I haven't done the same," Finn admitted. "I'm sorry about that. I'm going to do things differently from here on out."

Declan patted him on the back. "We're not keeping score, dude. You need us, we come. That's all."

Finn nodded, humbled by the show of affection, of loyalty. He'd never doubted it, but he'd never really thought about it either. "Tell everybody Merry Christmas. Give the kids hugs from me."

Ronan pulled him in for an embrace. "Tell them yourself when you call."

Finn laughed. Subtlety had never been Ronan's strong suit. "You got it."

He didn't know what the future held, for him and Elise or with regard to Isaac Fleming. But right now, in the company of his brothers, he knew he wouldn't face it alone.

20

Elise's stomach fluttered as she followed the maître d' through the restaurant. Finn walked behind her, and she thought again about the emerald green dress she'd bought especially for the occasion. Slinky and backless, it had been way too expensive, but she'd wanted their Christmas Eve dinner to be special, and she'd purchased a matching bra and panty set in the softest ivory lace she'd ever felt.

Now she wondered if the lace thong had been a mistake, if her panty line was visible under the silky dress, if Finn was watching her ass on the way to the table, if she wanted him to be watching her ass.

She didn't know if she was ready for any of this.

In her other life, before Manifest, she'd been to the finest restaurants in the world, had worn the most expensive clothes, ridden in the fastest cars with the richest men. Back then, she hadn't thought twice about whether she was dressed appropriately, whether she was beautiful, whether a man wanted her.

Now she felt uncertain, vulnerable in a way she had never felt back when she thought she'd had the world on a string, when she'd believed money and beautiful men and luxurious meals were the best the world had to offer.

The maître d' led them to the far end of a room with floor to ceiling windows and gestured to a table for two next to the glass. The restaurant, The Silver Darling, teetered at the edge of a peninsula, lights glittering on the water as barges and tankers eased their way in and out of Aberdeen harbor.

Across the inlet, houses hovered on a cliff, their lights dotting the darkness like stars. It felt like she and Finn were floating at the edge of the world, drifting toward the serene blackness of space.

Finn held out her chair and she sat down, her head rushing with dizziness as she inhaled his cologne, felt the brand of his hand on the bare skin at the small of her back before making his way to his seat across the table.

One of the waiters poured water into two empty

glasses. She took a drink while Finn got settled, taking in the way his shoulders pulled at the fabric of his dinner jacket, the sliver of bare skin that was visible between the open collar of a navy button-down that made his eyes look fiercely blue even in the candlelit restaurant.

He'd trimmed his beard, but it was still full, the wildness of it barely contained, a manicured jungle destined to win its fight with civility.

Heat bloomed from the pit of her stomach to her chest, spreading up her neck and onto her face until she had to resist the urge to fan herself with the menu that lay on the plate in front of her.

When she looked at Finn, she saw that he was watching her, his eyes locked with hers, a smile playing at the corners of his full mouth.

She smiled. "What?"

He shook his head. "Nothing."

"I feel like I have something on my face," she said.

"Your face is the point," he said. "I can't stop looking at you."

She took another drink of water, trying to cool the blood running like a river of lava in her veins. "You better stop. This is all going to go to my head."

He'd been speechless when she'd first appeared

in the flat in the green dress, had already told her she was exquisite, a word no man had ever used to describe in all the times she'd been described by men, which had been a lot.

"Good. You should know how beautiful you are." He picked up his menu, like he sensed the attention might be too much for her. "Let's order. I'm starving."

"Me too."

She was surprised to find she meant it. Since Ronan and Declan had left the day before, her whole body had come to life. She woke up early, energy buzzing in her veins, craving cold air on her face, wind in her hair.

She'd proceeded to devour half a loaf of bread standing at the counter in the flat's kitchen, toasting one piece after the other, washing it down with coffee. Then she'd dragged Finn outside to look at the holiday displays in store windows, imagining how she'd do them differently. She'd thought about Fringe, about what she would do if the store were hers, how she'd make the inventory younger and more bohemian.

She felt energized, awake, alive in a way she hadn't in a long, long time. If their time in Wales and

Cornwall had been about introspection, Scotland felt like the spark of rebirth.

She was starting to wonder if her previous malaise had something to do with Boston, with the sameness that had been her life and the people in it since her rescue. Maybe she'd needed it in the beginning, but now it felt like a too-tight dress, cutting off her circulation, making it hard to move.

Being alone with Finn felt like someone had taken wire cutters to the invisible ties that had been binding her for two years. The freedom was both shocking and exhilarating.

They conspired over the menu and ordered a feast of chilled oysters straight from the bay, seared squid with black olive dressing, halibut and smoked ham risotto, and duck with sour cherry sauce.

When Finn suggested wine, Elise agreed, even though it had been ages since she'd drank alcohol outside the house. In the bad old days, alcohol had made her even more impulsive, more reckless, than usual. Since her rescue, she'd been determined not to lose control, not to be foolish, ever again.

But she felt safe with Finn, knew he would never do anything to hurt her, that he would never let anyone else hurt her either.

After they'd ordered, Finn lifted his wine glass. "To Scotland and Christmas and us."

She smiled and echoed his words.

He set down his glass and seemed to hesitate. "Tell me about you, about your life," he finally said. "Before."

"Before," she echoed, feeling her way around the meaning of the word.

He reached for her hand. "If you want to, if it doesn't make you uncomfortable. I want to imagine you then, before I knew you."

Her mind flashed to nightclubs and loud music and endless drinks and the glowing dashboard of two-hundred-thousand-dollar cars.

"I was a twat. A total twat." She laughed. It felt good to say it out loud, to reduce her youthful aimlessness to such a simple word, a word that could apply to anyone at one time or another.

He grinned. "Tell me more."

She did. Over the flickering candlelight at the center of their table, she told him how ashamed she'd been of her upbringing, her single mom who always had a new boyfriend, who passed out drunk on the sofa while her friends from school had mothers who baked homemade cookies, who read them stories at night. She told him about food pantries and how cold it got in the winter when her mom forgot to pay the bill and the electric company shut off the heat, about her relief when her gramps had brought her and Julia to his house, which was always warm and cozy.

She'd wanted to be like everyone else. Like the friends from school who'd gone to college, who had clean-cut boyfriends with nice cars and good jobs, who posted about their perfect lives on social media. She'd wanted to prove that she was worthy too, that she was just as good.

Her mistake had been looking for everything she'd wanted in someone else, in the parade of men who were only different from the ones her mom had brought home because they were richer and more worldly, but who were just as inclined to use her and throw her away.

She thought she'd be ashamed, telling the truth about herself, but instead she felt a lightening inside her, the lifting of a weight she hadn't been aware she'd been carrying.

Finn listened without judgement, nodding in understanding when she talked about searching for the things she was missing, about running from herself before she'd figured out what an impossible task that was.

By the time they ordered coffee and a delicious creme brûlée spiced with cardamom and orange, she was almost euphoric. They finished dessert with their hands clasped across the table, the heat of Finn's gaze on her face heating her body in places she'd thought long dead.

They'd walked off their dinner on the cobblestone streets, deserted because of the holiday, surrounding the restaurant. The wind blowing in off the water was icy, but she was in no hurry to go back to the flat.

The night before, their first night without Ronan and Declan hadn't felt very different from all the nights they'd spent on the trip. She and Finn had busied themselves picking up a small, scraggly tree on the corner. They'd dragged it home and decorated it with decorations from a discount store two streets over, then ordered takeout and watched a Scottish game show on television while cuddling innocently on the couch before retiring to their individual rooms.

Nothing else seemed to be on the table for the evening, no pressure to advance their new relationship so soon after Ronan and Declan's departure.

Tonight felt different, the weight of Christmas and their solitude in the strange city and the intimate dinner lacing the air between them with anticipation. She felt like she was standing on the pier that stretched into the sea beyond the streets where they walked, like her toes were at the very edge, her body prepared for the shock of the water, walking the knife's edge of fear and excitement.

They took a car back to the flat. She watched the city pass on the other side of the glass, her hand warm in Finn's over the backseat between them. She tried not to think too hard about the moment when they'd walk into the flat, when Finn would help her with her coat, take off his own.

When they would either say goodnight or spend it together.

She tried to be in the present, like her therapist had instructed, tried to be in the car with the light-strung city casting its glow over the interior of the car, with Finn solid and sure next to her.

They stepped out of the car in front of the flat and wished the driver a Merry Christmas.

They rode the elevator in silence, and Elise stood nervously by while Finn unlocked the door, then stepped back to let her enter the flat ahead of him. It was dark except for the lights from their tiny tree. Elise walked toward it in the living room, her stomach fluttering as Finn hung their cold, damp coats near the door.

He walked toward her, his eyes liquid in the light from the Christmas tree. She held her breath as he placed his hands on her bare shoulders, his palms still cold enough to cause goosebumps to rise on her skin.

Or maybe that was just him. His nearness. His touch.

He brushed back a strand of her hair and took her face in his hands. It felt like it always felt, like she was something precious, like she was being held in ways she couldn't yet imagine.

She looked up at him, lost in his eyes, like mercury in the dim room. She didn't know what would happen next, didn't know if she wanted it to happen, if she would be able to bear it when it did.

If she would be able to bear it if it didn't.

He lowered his head and touched his lips to hers, pressing them tenderly against her mouth, his thumb stroking her jaw.

She wrapped her arms around his waist, relishing the hard planes of his body against the softness of her own, his broad chest, hard stomach, and muscled legs a delicious contrast to the swell of her breasts, the fleshy softness of her belly and thighs.

His tongue slipped into her mouth. She sighed and sank more fully against him as his tongue made slow sweeps, its motion languid, almost lazy, as if he were in no hurry when every nerve in her body was sizzling, crackling like live wires desperate for connection.

She met the exploration of his tongue with her own. His shaft was hard in his trousers, and heat blossomed at her core, spreading outward to the far reaches of her body until she was desperate to feel his bare skin against her own, to feel the slide of his body, the completion as he filled her.

Her body trembled with need, her nipples hard, panties wet between her legs.

She was so lost in sensation, she almost didn't realize he'd broken the kiss. He leaned his forehead against hers and she was surprised to find the only sound in the room was her own heavy breathing.

He stared into her eyes, his own breathing calm and measured as the moment stretched thin.

Take me to bed. Take off my clothes. Take my body. Take my heart.

Take it all.

The words stuck in her throat.

He kissed her cheek and stepped away. When he spoke, his voice was low and hoarse. "Thank you for a lovely evening."

He walked down the hall and disappeared into his bedroom. She was still trembling when the shower started a minute later.

21

Finn stepped into the shower and tipped his head under the spray of hot water. Any other night, he would sigh with relief, let the water wash away the tightness in his body.

Tonight there was no such relief. Tonight the tightness in his body was a result not of worry or physical stress but of the discipline that had been required of him to kiss Elise, to touch her and to walk away.

And he'd had to walk away. If he wanted their relationship to progress in any meaningful, healthy way, in any way that wouldn't be traumatizing for her, he had to be very careful as they navigated the physical part of their relationship.

She still hadn't gone into detail about what had

happened to her at the hands of Manifest, but he could guess.

In his worst nightmares, he could guess.

So far she hadn't flinched when he'd reached for her hand, when he'd held her on the sofa while they watched a movie, when he'd kissed her. In fact, if he hadn't known about her past, he would never guess what lurked there.

But he did know, and he had to be prepared for the possibility that every step they took toward intimacy would be a landmine that would blow to bits the expanding but fragile foundation of their relationship.

He'd settled on a plan of taking things slow, letting her lead, making sure when — if — the physical aspect of their relationship advanced, it would be because she wanted him as badly as he wanted her.

Except he hadn't counted on the discipline it would require of him once Ronan and Declan left Scotland. They'd spent nearly two weeks traveling together, and while Finn's physical attraction to Elise had grown right along with the deeper feelings of attachment he had for her, it had been tempered by the proximity of his brothers.

His imagination had been let loose with their

absence, and he'd spent the last two days imagining various scenarios in which he ended up naked with Elise, his hands roaming her body, his mouth tasting every inch of her.

He groaned into the water and picked up the soap, working around his still-erect cock until its throbbing wouldn't allow him to ignore it a second longer.

He took his shaft in his hand and squeezed, stifling the moan that rose to his lips when he imagined it as Elise's hand, her palm silky and soft.

He pictured her in the green dress, imagined sliding the straps off her shoulders, watching the dress fall to the floor, her naked body revealed to him over the pool of emerald silk.

She would be perfect for him. He knew that already, saw it in the line of her breasts under the thin fabric of the dress, her elegant back, visible in the dress and begging for his hand, the swell of her ass when she walked.

He stroked his shaft as he imagined stepping naked toward her, taking her in his arms, his tongue sliding into the sweet pool of her mouth as she took him in her hand.

She would stroke him slowly at first, taking her time, while he kissed his way down her neck and chest. When he took one of her nipples in his mouth, she would moan and throw her head back. Her long hair would skim his hands, squeezing the soft, firm pillows of her ass.

He would suck her nipple to a hard peak and slide one hand between her legs, part the lips of her pussy with his fingers, slide them into her wet, slippery heat. She would stroke him with more urgency, gasping as he circled her clit with his thumb.

He could almost hear her breath coming in short, shallow gasps. Could almost hear her begging him to take her as he stroked his own flesh, expanding in his hand, growing heavier with the force of his need.

He would lift her off her feet, feel the heat of her core against his stomach as she wrapped her legs around his waist. He would carry her to bed and lay her down. She would reach for him, make it clear that she wanted him.

He saw himself spreading her legs, looking down at her perfect pussy, seeing moisture glistening like a mirage, the sweetest kind of oasis.

His orgasm built as he imagined positioning himself between her thighs, the head of his cock sensitive as it rubbed against her center, the promise of release stretching his desire into an almost unendurable pleasure.

He saw her face, delicate and beautiful, her eyes half-open as she looked at him, begging him to take her.

He plunged into her all at once, pushing through the wet fire of her pussy until every inch of him was buried inside her, her body clamped down on his shaft, squeezing and…

He groaned as he came, exploding onto the shower wall, light flashing behind his eyelids as his body released its pent-up tension. He imagined plunging into her again and again, his body shuddering as he spilled everything into the hot steam of the shower, imagining he was spilling it into her, that she was coming with him, crying out into the room as her body rocked with his.

When he was spent, he sagged against the tile, his breath coming fast, his body loose and suddenly tired.

Would it be the way he imagined when he was finally able to be that close to Elise, when he was finally able to be inside her? Would she want him as much as he wanted her? Would he make a mistake and scare her?

It was the last thought that almost broke him.

She'd begged him not to pity her, not to try and protect her, but when he thought about her — shower fantasies aside — protecting her was all he wanted to do.

Except the only way to do that, to protect her from him, from the inevitable pain of him leaving, was to walk away now.

And god help him, he couldn't.

He couldn't.

22

Elise stood at the window of the flat and watched as Finn exited the building and started up the street. His shoulders, ensconced in his peacoat, were still unmistakably broad from a distance, and she felt her pulse quicken as she took in his confident stride. He was a man who was perfectly comfortable in the world even when he didn't know where it would take him. A man who would rise to any occasion, who could handle anything.

Even after a week alone, she still couldn't stop looking at him.

He stopped on the corner, waiting for the light to change, then continued up the street, heading for the market to pick up some supplies for New Year's

Eve the following day. She'd wanted to go with him — she always wanted to be with him — but she also wanted to check in with Aliyah and Julia.

She and Finn had been cocooned in their own world since Ronan and Declan had left. They'd spent a quiet Christmas opening gifts — she'd gotten him a Shetland scarf and a travel journal, he'd gotten her a small Shield Knot pendant, a Scottish symbol of protection, suspended on a thin gold chain — and cooking an elaborate feast. They'd eaten in their pajamas on the sofa, the room lit by their tree while they watched It's a Wonderful Life.

They'd spent every day since in much the same way: eating leftovers and takeout, watching old movies, taking long walks that numbed their cheeks, their cuddles on the couch turning more passionate as the days passed, Elise's hunger for him growing to a fever pitch she knew she wouldn't be able to deny much longer.

She'd spoken to Julia on Christmas, but the conversation had been anything but private. Finn had been sitting next to her in the flat, and Elise had been able to hear the cacophony of the Murphy house at Christmas in the background, JT and Griffin chattering up a storm, Declan and Kate debating something having to do with chocolate soufflé, someone's Christmas playlist a backdrop to it all.

She and Julia had had a pleasant enough conversation, but she'd sensed her sister's unasked questions, her concern seeping across the miles.

Elise stepped away from the window and went to the kitchen to put water on for tea. She would ease into her phone calls by calling Aliyah first, checking on her friend and the store, filling her in about Finn.

Then she would deal with Julia.

She set the phone on the counter while it rang and used the time to pull a mug down from the cabinet.

Aliyah picked up on the second ring. "Well, well, well! If it isn't my prodigal store manager!"

Elise laughed. "I know, I know. I'm sorry I haven't been in touch before now."

"Don't be sorry," Aliyah said. "Just tell me every dirty detail."

Elise spooned tea into the mug and scooted onto the countertop, her legs dangling over the tile floor. "Not a lot of dirty details. Not yet anyway. How are you?"

"I'm fine, girl. Nothing much has changed since you left, unless you count the inventory at the store."

"Really?" The kettle began to whistle and Elise poured hot water into her mug. "Is it William? Is he changing things already?"

"Oh, he's changing things alright," Aliyah said.

"I take it they're not good changes?" Elise asked.

Aliyah sighed. "It's not bad exactly. It's just... fast fashion. You know?"

"Oh no... really?" Bonnie hadn't exactly had her finger on the pulse of youthful trends, but she'd tried to order a fair amount of stock from small designers and companies that produced their clothing ethically.

"Yeah. I'm pretty sure everything we carry now was made in a sweatshop in Cambodia or Vietnam," Aliyah said.

Elise's heart sank. She'd always taken pride in the fact that Fringe's stock was more ethically sourced than the inventory in big-box stores. If it had been her store, she would have taken it further, sourcing from female-owned co-ops and suppliers around the world, but she'd admired Bonnie's efforts at doing business in a responsible manner.

"That sucks," Elise said. It was an understatement, but she didn't have anything else on such short notice. She carried her tea into the living room and sat on the sofa. "How's the new boss?"

"As hot as ever. That accent gets me hot and bothered."

Elise analyzed Aliyah's voice for something left unsaid, but there didn't seem to be any subtext. It was enough to make Elise wonder if she'd imagined her own strange encounter with William Pearson. "Is he single?"

"How would I know?" Aliyah asked. "The guy might be hot but he's got a stick up his ass the size of Texas."

Elise laughed.

"Seriously," Aliyah continued. "He's nice to look at, but bedside manner isn't his strong suit."

"Any idea what the long-term plan is for the store?" It seemed like something she should ask, even though the store and all her associated thoughts and concerns seemed a million miles away.

"Not really," Aliyah said. "He has asked about you though, about when you're coming back."

"Really? Did he seem pissed?" Elise waited for the familiar job-related anxiety to hit her, the fear that one of the few things she had in her life, one of the few things that made her feel like a normal person, might be taken from her.

But it didn't, and she filed it away to think about later.

"Not pissed exactly. Just... concerned. I think he's worried you won't come back."

"I don't know why that would worry him," Elise said. "You're perfectly capable of taking over for me."

"You think?" Aliyah's uncertainty was obvious even over the phone.

"I know. You're running things now, aren't you?"

"I guess so, but I don't want the job," Aliyah said. "Not if it means you're not working there. You're the only thing that makes it fun. Who else would make fun of the bad inventory with me?" She hesitated. "I mean, you are coming back, right?"

"Of course." Elise didn't hesitate. Her job at Fringe didn't include a corner office or a fat salary, but she felt competent there. She felt in control. Besides, what else would she do?

"Whew," Aliyah said. "Good. So?"

"So what?" Elise asked, reaching for her tea.

"Don't be coy! Tell me about your trip. Never mind, you can tell me about the trip when you get back. Tell me about the guy! Is he still hot? Do you still like him after being around him 24/7? Have you done the deed?"

Elise laughed. "Um... let's see: yes, yes, and no. Unfortunately on the last one?"

"Unfortunately?"

Elise could picture Aliyah sitting at her tiny kitchen table, her eyebrows raised in question.

Elise sighed. "Yeah, I think so. I mean, I'm nervous about..."

"Doing the deed?" Aliyah supplied.

"It'll be the first time since everything that..." She took a deep breath. "Since everything that happened to me." She thought about all the moments between her and Finn since Ronan and Declan had left for the States, all the times she'd longed for Finn's touch only to watch him drop his hand or pull her into a cozy but chaste hug, all the times she'd watched him walk to his room before retiring to her own, the hours she'd spent tossing and turning, her body aching with need. "But yeah, I think I want to."

"So what's the hold up?" Aliyah's voice was gentle.

"Originally, it was me — I said I wanted to take it slow — but now I think he's just being careful. He doesn't want me to feel rushed or pressured or whatever, so we just kiss and cuddle and make out and stuff."

"And you feel okay when you do that stuff?" Aliyah asked.

"I feel surprisingly okay. If anything, I keep wishing he'd just make the move," Elise said.

"You don't have to wait for him," Aliyah said.

Elise bit her lip. "That's true, I guess."

"You're probably right. He wants to be sure you're ready, but how can he be sure if you don't tell him?" Aliyah asked.

"So you think I should just..." Elise laughed. "Tear his clothes off?"

"Well, yeah. Or you could just tell him you're ready. Like, you appreciate that he's been so patient, but you're over patient," Aliyah said.

Elise wasn't so sure. She was still getting her head around wanting Finn, around the fact that all the parts of her body she had assumed were dead had been brought back to life by her desire for him.

Telling him how she felt, how much she wanted him, was next-level surrender.

"How do I know for sure?" Elise hated how small and scared her voice sounded. "How do I know that once we start I won't freak out and change my mind?"

"So what if you do?" Aliyah asked. "You're allowed to change your mind at any point, and if Finn is half the man you think he is, half the man you deserve, he'll be cool with it. Right?"

"Right." Elise didn't have to think about the

answer. She knew Finn would be okay with it, that he'd support her no matter what.

So why was she still so scared?

23

"Is it too soon for champagne?"

Finn looked up from the sofa. Elise stood on the threshold to the living room, holding one of the two bottles of Veuve Clicquot he'd bought for the occasion. "It's never too soon for champagne on New Year's Eve."

"My thoughts exactly." She came around the sofa and set the glasses on the coffee table.

He studied her as she worked the cork on the bottle. He was used to seeing her in flannel pajama bottoms and big T-shirts, an ensemble that had proven shockingly erotic during their time in Scotland.

She'd looked exquisite at dinner in another killer dress, this time a slinky gold affair with a plunging neckline that had made it difficult to enjoy the food at the Michelin-starred restaurant he'd chosen. When they'd gotten back to the flat for their quiet New Year's Eve, they'd gone their separate ways to change.

Finn had braced himself for the oblivious sexiness of Elise in her usual nighttime attire only to see her emerge in a black silk nightgown with a matching robe. It slipped off her shoulder, revealing the slim black straps of the nightgown as she worked the cork loose from the champagne bottle.

He had a flash of his fingers pushing the strap off her shoulder, the nightgown falling to the floor in a soft rush, her body suddenly — gloriously — naked before him.

His cock jumped to attention in his sweat pants and he shifted on the couch, trying to focus on the champagne Elise poured into the glasses, the bubbles catching the light from the Christmas tree, still lit in the corner, instead of the all too familiar passion simmering in his blood.

She handed him one of the glasses, raised her own, and licked her lips. "To Scotland. And to… getting closer and closer."

A flush spread over her cheeks and he was torn

between wanting to hold her and wanting to strip her naked and drive into her then and there.

"Amen," he said.

The days since Christmas had been an exercise in restraint, hour after hour holding Elise's hand during long walks through the city, laying on the sofa with her body pressed to his while they watched a movie, feeling her mouth open as the passion between them grew.

Every minute had been the sweetest kind of torment. He relished every second of being close to her, but it only made him want more.

He drank from his champagne glass, watching as Elise drank from her own, her slim throat rippling as she swallowed.

He took the glass from her hand and set it on the coffee table, then pulled her onto his lap. The lush softness of her ass sent another rocket of lust through his body, and he wrapped his arms around her waist and touched his lips to hers, trying to focus on how much he cared about the woman in his arms — which was a lot — instead of how much he wanted her.

Which was also a lot.

She tightened her arms around his neck and opened her mouth wider, her tongue hot and urgent against his own. There was nothing timid in her kiss, nothing to hint at hesitation. He wanted to believe it meant something, but he didn't dare. He focused on the kiss instead, on how good it felt to hold her, on how happy it made him to be with her even if they never made it to bed together.

She broke the kiss and he tried to hide his surprise when she turned in his lap until she was straddling him, her breasts pressed against his chest, his cock nestled into the heat at her core.

Fuck. He shouldn't have changed into sweatpants. At least in trousers he had a little help keeping everything contained.

Her eyes were bottomless as she held his gaze. "I want to be with you, Finn. Tonight. Now."

They were words he'd longed to hear, but he couldn't allow his eagerness to override his feelings for her. "Are you sure? Because there's no pressure, El. Tonight is special just because we're here, alone together. That's all I need."

She cupped his face in her hands and kissed him long and slow. "I'm sure," she said against his lips. "Now take me to bed, Finn Murphy."

He groaned and cupped her ass cheeks, gloriously bare in the thong panties under her nightgown, then lay her back on the sofa.

His mind felt like it was short-circuiting, his body clamoring for release at the sight of her while his brain told him to take it slow, not to hurt her, not to go too fast, but also not to make her feel like he was trying to protect her, something he'd promised not to do.

He used the time to drink her in. She'd let down her hair after they'd gotten home from dinner, and it was spread out in a halo of gold that shone in the light from the Christmas tree. One arm was flung over her head, her breasts barely covered by the silky black fabric of the nightgown. Her knees were bent, legs partially open for him, the cleft between her legs hidden in inviting shadow.

"Jesus, Elise," he said, his voice gruff. "You're so fucking beautiful."

She reached for him. "Show me, Finn."

He stretched out over her body, easing his weight on top of her and supporting as much of it as he could on his forearms, not wanting to crush her. He brushed the hair back from her forehead and looked down at her, his chest filling with an emotion he didn't recognize.

Her eyes were like amber fire. "Don't be gentle with me, Finn. I don't want that. Not this time."

Her words fanned the flames already raging

inside him, and he crushed her mouth under his, invading it with his tongue. His hands traveled her body, alternating between the silk of her nightgown and the satiny smoothness of her skin.

He resisted the urge to tear it off, to drive into her then and there. Being told not to be gentle was one thing: doing what he really wanted to do to her, a woman who'd sparked powerful and unfamiliar emotions in him, was something else.

She writhed under him as he kissed his way across her jaw and down her neck. Her hands reached for the hem of his shirt, and he broke contact with her skin long enough for her to pull it off.

This was good. However painful it was for him to take it slow, it was preferable to the possibility of making a mistake, of scaring her or setting back their relationship.

She tossed the shirt aside and he settled back on top of her, kissing the hollow at the base of her throat and touching his lips to her chest, traveling toward her breasts.

She slid her hands into his hair, fisting locks of it in her fingers. It tugged at his scalp, providing an erotic shot of pleasure pain.

He nudged aside the nightgown to reveal a

perfect pink nipple. He sucked in a breath and lowered his mouth, touching his tongue to the hard little bud. He circled it, wanting to make sure it was okay. When she didn't object he drew into his mouth and gently sucked.

She gasped, her back arching off the sofa, her fingers tightening in his hair.

"Finn..."

He worked the nipple with his tongue while he sucked, slipping one of his hands into the nightgown and covering her other breast with his palm, gently squeezing the nipple between his thumb and forefinger.

"Oh, god..." she moaned.

His cock felt like it was going to tear free of his sweatpants, the pressure so intense he worried he might come without ever having been inside her.

She lifted her hips off the couch, locking her calves behind his ankles, her hands trailing down his back. His shaft was wedged between her legs, the heat from her core seeping through his sweatpants.

She reached for his waistband, slid one hand into his sweats, and wrapped her palm around his throbbing shaft.

Light flashed behind his eyes and he lifted his mouth from her breast, groaning as she stroked him.

He kissed his way down her stomach over her ribcage and the soft swell of her lower stomach, if only to distract himself, to distract her from the rhythmic motion of her hand on his shaft.

He sat back on his heels and looked down at her. The nightgown had slid up around her hips, revealing the pale skin of her thighs, the tiny black underwear that covered her mound. He was dying to rip them off, bury his face in the sweetness of her sex, lick and lap until she came against his mouth.

He bent over her and pushed them aside instead, drawing in his breath at the sight of her sex. He could imagine plunging into her, the sweet slide as he pushed through the swollen tunnel of her pussy.

He ran his thumb over her glistening folds and bent to slide his tongue inside her.

"Finn... can we...?"

He looked up at her. "Anything."

"Can we not do that yet?" Her brow was furrowed, her eyes clouded with doubt.

"We can do — and not do — anything you want." He hated that his voice was hoarse, didn't know if it was from desire or emotion. He stretched out over her body again and kissed her. "I'll tell you what: you show me. Show me what you want, El."

He rolled her on top of him, stifling a moan

when his cock pressed tight against her damp panties, separated from the paradise of her pussy by a tiny strip of fabric he could have torn away in less than two seconds.

It went against his nature to give her control — he had always been the dominant one in bed — but it was the only way he could be sure. The only way he would know everything they did was something she wanted.

Doubt shaded her features. "I don't know — "

He lifted his hips, pressed up into the warmth of her pussy. "You know, El. Listen to your body. Show me what you want, or don't. Kiss me and let me just hold you instead. It's your call."

He held his breath, wondering if she'd change her mind, if they'd moved too fast after all, if she hadn't been ready.

She lifted the hem of her nightgown and stripped it off, tossing it aside. Then she lowered her mouth to his, her breasts pressed flat against his bare chest as her tongue slipped between his lips.

24

She didn't want to stop. She knew she could, knew Finn wouldn't mind even though she'd felt the press of his erection since she'd first sat in his lap, had felt it countless times over the days they'd spent alone in Scotland.

But she wanted him. She wanted his company and his heart and his soul, and yes, his body too, for as long as she could have them.

It was the only thing she was sure about.

She savored the warmth of his bare skin against hers, the hard plane of his muscled chest against her bare breasts erotic in a way she hadn't expected. She angled her head to take their kiss deeper, heat sparking between her legs as he met the sweeps and thrusts of her tongue with his own.

His beard caused delicious friction against her jaw, and his cock was hard between her thighs, pressing against her aroused sex. Her hips moved of their own accord, picking up a rhythm in their kiss that was beyond thought, beyond reason.

He held her head in his hands, and she wondered if it was because he was afraid to touch her, afraid it would be too much.

But no, when her eyes fluttered open, he was looking at her, emotion so raw on his face she had to look away.

She kissed his chest, lingering over the rise of his chiseled pecs, making her way down the corded muscle of his abs. After weeks of stealing glances at him, studying him when she thought he wasn't looking, imagining his body under jeans and trousers, button-downs and T-shirts, it was a luxury to have his skin under her mouth and fingertips, to have every inch of him at her disposal.

His stomach rippled when she positioned herself between his thighs and tugged at his waistband. He looked down at her with naked desire, his eyes half closed.

He hadn't been wearing underwear, and his cock sprung free as she pulled the sweatpants over his hips, down his lean but muscular legs.

She dropped them on the floor and looked at him, need crackling like fire through her veins. He was massive, thick and beautifully formed, rigid and engorged.

"I'm not going to be able to control myself if you keep looking at me like that," he said, his voice low and hoarse.

"Sorry," she said.

He reached for her hand. "Don't be sorry. I like knowing you want me, that you want this."

She licked her lips, contemplated taking him in her mouth, then positioned her body over it instead, straddling his hips with her thighs.

One step at a time.

"I want you." She leaned over him, ran her tongue along the seam of his lips until he groaned and clutched her ass. "I want this."

She pushed her panties aside and slid her pussy, wet and throbbing, over his shaft, soaking it with her juices.

He squeezed her ass. "Fuck, El..." Her panties sprang back into place, blocking their skin-to-skin contact. "Want me to get rid of those for you?"

"Yes," she gasped.

She heard a brief rip, felt him toss the offending fabric aside.

"That's better," he murmured, lifting his head and sucking on one of her nipples.

She tipped her head back, lost in sensation: Finn's mouth, warm and insistent, tugging on her nipple, sending a rocket of urgency to her center as she slid back and forth over his shaft.

His tip bumped against her clit, stoking the orgasm that had been lurking at her center since he'd pulled her into his lap.

"I want you, Finn. I want you so much." She could barely get the words out around her need for him.

"Then take me, sweetheart. I'm all yours."

She rose onto her knees and was positioning herself over him when she realized they'd never discussed protection.

"Do you want a condom? I'm on the pill." It hadn't been about sex when she'd decided to take the pill. It had been the knowledge that of all the terrible things that had happened to her, she'd dodged one very big bullet. It had been about taking control of her body, making sure no one could ever fire that gun at her again. "I haven't been with anyone, but we can... if you want..."

"No," he said. "Not unless you want it. I'm clean."

She took him in her hand and guided him to her

entrance. "I want to really feel you, if that's okay with you."

What had happened to her with Manifest had been intimate, but it hadn't been personal. She wanted it to be personal with Finn. Wanted to know it was him inside her.

"It's more than okay," he said.

She hovered over the head of his cock, then lowered herself slowly onto him, sighing as he slid into her an inch at a time. It took forever for him to fill her, and she held her breath as his thick crown parted her swollen tunnel, pushing through her until he came to rest against her cervix.

She relaxed her muscles and he sunk another inch into her.

She waited, half-expecting an assault of memory to invade the moment. But there was only him: Finn. The man who'd brought her body and heart back to life.

Sighing, she leaned over to kiss him. He parted her lips with his tongue. The slide of it into her mouth wasn't unlike the feeling of him filling her pussy, and her hips rocked against him, her clit grinding against his stomach.

Her breath was already coming fast and shallow, the knot at her core unraveling with the friction on the bundle of nerves at her center, the surge of him inside her.

She lifted her hips, sighing as she dragged herself slowly off him, gasping when she dropped onto him again, this time hard and fast.

"You feel so good, El. So fucking good." Finn held onto her hips, but he was letting her do all the work, and she knew he was letting her take the lead, wanting her to take what she wanted the way she wanted it.

She moved faster, rocking her hips over his, marveling at the perfection of their fit, the way her body expanded around him, enveloping him like a glove that had been made for him long before they ever met.

He moved with her, caught up in the moment, lifting his hips to meet her on the downward motion, pulling back when she slid off him, pushing down on her hips to drive into her again.

The orgasm built inside her, filling her stomach and spreading outward until her limbs tingled. She moved faster, chasing the release, beyond thought as she worked to meet the primal demand of her body.

"Let it go," Finn said. "Come for me, El."

The words were like a firebomb, setting off an explosion that came all at once, tipping her over the edge, pitching her into a light-filled oblivion that shook her body so violently she cried out.

He let loose a groan that bordered on a growl, an animal sound that seemed to vibrate through her as he came.

She shuddered around him, her body clamping down on his shaft as the tremors rolled over and through her, obliterating everything but the pure ecstasy of the release, the feel of Finn spilling into her as he let go too.

The orgasm seemed to go on forever, a series of waves that left her gasping and limp, draped over Finn's body.

He wrapped his arms around her and kissed her bare shoulder. "You good?"

She nodded against his chest. "Hmm-mm. Better than good. Are you?"

"I'd be better if we could stay like this forever."

The word rang through her heart.

Forever.

It was something they wouldn't have, something Finn, the prodigal son with a wandering soul, a man who couldn't commit to a single place on the planet, wasn't built for.

He rolled onto his side, taking her with him until she was stretched out next to him on the sofa. In the distance, bells rang out from a church downtown, the muffled thud of fireworks exploding in the skies beyond the flat.

He stroked the hair back from her forehead and looked down at her. "Happy New Year, El."

She smiled up at him. "Happy New Year."

She'd suffered years of misery, of pain that had seemed unending and inescapable. For once, she wanted to be only here, to enjoy the moment when Finn Murphy was still hers.

25

Finn opened his eyes, taking a minute to adjust to the light leaking into the bedroom from the terrace doors before turning to look at Elise, asleep in his arms.

His heart stuttered at the sight of her: the sweep of her eyelashes against the creamy skin of her cheek, her hair tangled on his pillow, her lips parted in sleep. She looked so peaceful, so young without the worry that lurked behind her eyes. The urge to protect her rushed at him like a rogue wave, stealing his breath.

He would kill anyone who tried to hurt her, wanted to hunt the men who already had, wanted to watch their lives slip away under his hands.

His anger scared him, bringing him too close to

the philosophical differences that had kept him away from his brothers. He wasn't like them. He didn't kill people, not even people who deserved it. Justice was for the legal system, and for whatever higher power existed in a world that too often seemed ruled by chaos and pain.

His thoughts released a manic burst of energy, and he eased out from under Elise, not wanting to wake her, and padded naked into the living room.

He smiled at the sight of their clothes strewn across the living room floor. They'd taken the bottle of champagne to his bedroom, celebrating the new year with another round of lovemaking. It had been slower than the first time, although Elise had still kept him from using his mouth to make her come.

He didn't know why it was off-limits, but it didn't matter. It had been a kind of nirvana just to touch her naked body, to feel her hands on his own, to drive into her and watch the flush spread across her chest as she approached orgasm, to feel her pussy tighten around him while she came, to hold her in his arms all night long.

"Fuck," he muttered, realizing he was hard again.

He slid on his sweatpants and made his way to the kitchen to start the coffee. When it was brewing, the scent filling the air with earthy goodness, he removed a pan from under the cabinet, trying not to make too much noise.

When he rose with it in his hand, Elise was standing in the doorway, naked, a smile playing at the corners of her mouth. "Good morning."

"Damn. Did I wake you?" His gaze combed her body. "Also, damn. Forget breakfast."

He dropped the pan on the stove and walked toward her, pulling her into his arms. She was soft and warm, sinking into him, pressing against his hard-on.

"I woke up because I felt you were gone." She reached into his sweats and squeezed his shaft. "But now that I'm here, I want breakfast."

He groaned and kissed her before turning back to the stove. "If the lady wants breakfast, the lady gets breakfast."

She walked to the coffee pot and poured two cups. She set one next to him on the stove, then hopped onto the counter.

He looked at her, the beauty of her nakedness still a gut punch. "That doesn't seem safe." He grinned. "For me, I mean."

She set down her coffee and laughed, then slid off the counter. "Fine. Spoilsport."

He watched her walk to the living room and

bend over to pick up her nightgown, her lush ass spreading to give him a perfect view of her pussy.

"Jesus christ," he muttered.

His desire for her was like an eternal fucking flame.

She slipped the nightgown over her head while she walked back into the kitchen. "Better?"

"Safer," he said.

She grinned and slid back onto the counter, watching as he removed bacon and eggs from the fridge. He went to work whipping them up for an omelette, digging around for some mushrooms, fresh tarragon, and some of the Anster they'd bought at a little cheese shop the weekend before.

He dropped a big hunk of fresh butter into the hot pan and swirled it around before adding the mushrooms and tarragon. He added bacon to another skillet.

"That smells so good." Elise said. "I'm starving."

"Good. I'm going to feed you double so I can take you back to bed."

She laughed. "I won't say no."

While the mushrooms cooked, he sliced two pieces of crusty bread from the bakery down the street and put them in the toaster. Then he slid the eggs into the pan on top of the mushrooms and turned the bacon.

It took him a minute to place the feeling building inside him. When he did he realized it was contentment. He'd had bursts of happiness in his travels — plenty of them in fact, times when he'd realized that while everyone else was in an office he was standing at the base of a pyramid or on top of a mountain, times when he'd looked around and realized a group of people he'd started out not knowing at all had become something like family.

But contentment... that had been in short supply. It wasn't something he'd expected to find in a flat in Scotland, cooking breakfast for a woman.

And that was the rub: Elise wasn't just any woman, something he'd sensed the first time they'd talked on the patio in Boston. He couldn't help being intrigued by the realization.

He buttered the toast and was sliding the eggs onto two plates when his phone buzzed from the counter. He wiped his hands before picking it up to read the text from Ronan.

Happy New Year. Have news on Fleming. Arriving in five hours.

26

Elise pushed the cart through the grocery store, absent-mindedly adding stuff, her mind on the text from Ronan and his impending arrival with Declan. It felt a little like being a teenager whose parents were returning after a weekend away, and she and Finn had gone to work splitting the tasks, Finn tidying the flat while Elise stocked the fridge. She didn't know how long Ronan and Declan planned to stay — she didn't even know how long she and Finn would be in Scotland — but she knew the Murphy men drank a lot of coffee and ate a lot of food.

She stopped at the cheese counter, her gaze sweeping the selection. News of Ronan and Declan's return had ever so slightly shifted the atmosphere between her and Finn. It was a reminder that their time together wasn't unlimited, that it was dependent on what happened with Fleming, and they'd eaten breakfast mostly in silence, her bare feet on top of his under the table, his hand reaching for hers like he was afraid she would disappear.

She shook her head, wondering how long she'd been staring into space. She chose a couple of cheeses she'd never tried and pushed the cart toward the butcher's counter.

Her stomach was a bundle of nerves. Was it because she was worried for Finn and the news about Fleming? Or because of what that news would mean for their relationship?

Maybe both.

She wanted Finn to have closure, but she knew that closure meant an end to whatever it was they'd been building. She allowed herself to imagine another outcome: Finn staying in Boston, building a life with her there. Or alternatively, Elise leaving everything behind, joining him on whatever adventure he had next.

Except she couldn't imagine Finn staying in Boston. She couldn't imagine Finn staying anywhere. Not yet anyway. Whatever he'd been looking for on the road, he hadn't finished with it yet.

Leaving the States herself was almost as unimaginable. Until the last three weeks, she couldn't even walk in an unfamiliar neighborhood in Boston without having an anxiety attack, couldn't see a strange man in the grocery store without wanting to run. How could she leave behind everything she knew, step into a life that would be unfamiliar and terrifying every second of the day?

And then there was the other thing, the biggest thing of all: Finn hadn't asked her to join him.

For a man as accustomed to solitude as Finn, it would be akin to asking her to marry him. A big step and probably not one he would be ready to take anytime soon.

She asked the butcher to wrap four thick steaks, took the package from him, and made her way quickly through the rest of the store. She was anxious to get back to the flat, to get back to Finn. They'd showered together before she'd left the apartment, making love under the hot water, and she'd marveled that she could still want him so much, that she could open to him like a blooming flower when for so long she'd felt withered and dead.

Her body quickened at the thought of him pushing into her, his tongue invading her mouth while his cock invaded her core. They wouldn't have time for any more of that, but if she hurried, they might have time to cuddle on the couch before Ronan and Declan turned up.

She finished the shopping and stood in line to pay, then carried the bags outside.

It was still cold, but the sky was a clear cerulean, the sun so bright it was almost blinding. She set the bags down long enough to fish her sunglasses out of her pocket and slide her cap over her head, glad she'd left her hair down for extra warmth.

She looked up at the sky while she walked. The sun was like a benediction, a message from the universe that everything would be okay, that the new year ahead would be full of light instead of darkness.

It was optimistic given the situation with Finn, but she could use a little optimism.

She waited at the corner for the light to change, shifting the heavy bags in her arms. Other than her mom and her sister, her nephew, and the Murphy family, she didn't miss much about her life in Boston, but she definitely missed having a car to take grocery shopping.

The light changed and she stepped into the crosswalk and headed for the flat. By the time she approached the door to the flat's lobby, she was feeling better, her spirits buoyed by the walk and the sun.

"There you are."

She spun around at the sound of the voice and spotted Ronan pulling a bag from the back of a Range Rover.

"You made it!" she said.

"We made it." He closed the trunk and walked toward her with the bag in one hand.

He looked down at her, and for a minute she thought he would say something, something about her and Finn. Instead he took one of the bags and started for the door. "Let's talk. And eat. I'm starving."

27

Finn sat across from Ronan and Declan, tuning out the buzz of the other people dining and drinking in the pub around them. He hadn't wanted to come, had preferred to stay at the flat and learn why Ronan and Declan had rushed back to Scotland, but Ronan had been too hungry to wait for them to cook the food Elise had brought home.

It was typical of Ronan, used to having things exactly the way he wanted them, which was how Finn found himself tapping his foot under the table waiting for his brothers to get to the fucking point.

"So?" Finn looked pointedly at Ronan. "Are you sufficiently nourished? Comfortable? Warm enough? Or do you need a nap before we talk?"

"Don't be a smartass," Ronan said, wiping his

mouth and pushing the plate holding the remains of his steak pie. "When we tell you why we're here, you're going to thank us for coming at all."

"Then how about you tell me?" Finn asked through clenched teeth.

Ronan leaned back in the booth and took a long drink of his beer. Now he was just fucking with Finn, but drawing attention to it would only make it worse, something Finn knew from a lifetime of being the youngest brother to an obnoxious oldest.

Finn cut a glance at Declan, but one look told him if he was looking for backup from Dec, he was barking up the wrong tree. Slouched in the booth, his gaze roaming the small wood-paneled pub, Declan looked perfectly at ease and not at all in a hurry.

Elise was silent beside Finn, not that he would have involved her anyway. He'd barely had time to register the potential impact of his brothers' surprise visit on his relationship with Elise, but he knew he didn't want it to end.

Ronan had studied them both when he'd stepped into the flat, like he'd been trying to calculate the progress of their relationship over the holiday. Finn hoped his insistence on including Elise in their conversation at the pub settled any remaining questions. He wouldn't be home forever, but he planned to be with Elise while he was, and he didn't plan to keep any secrets.

Anything they said to him, they could say in front of her.

"Remember how we couldn't figure out why a geologist, a lab nerd, would be in Ukraine with a bunch of mercenaries?" Ronan finally asked.

"Yeah?"

"We figured out why," Ronan said.

"And? Are you going to tell me or should we waste another hour while I guess for your amusement?"

"He's working for someone else," Declan said. "Or not someone, exactly, but something."

"Who?" Finn asked.

"Ever hear of the Omni Group?" Ronan asked.

"Aren't there a thousand companies called the Omni Group?" Finn asked. It was one of those generic company names that were interchangeable with a thousand other generic company names. Finn had always wondered if they were designed to make people forget them.

"Maybe," Ronan said. "But we're only interested in the one Fleming has been working for."

"What's he doing for them?" Finn asked, hoping to cut to the chase.

Declan took a drink of his beer. "We don't know yet. We assume Fleming signed an NDA."

"Then how do you know he's working for the Omni Group?" Finn asked.

"The charter Fleming used when he took that last trip is owned by Omni, so we had Clay track all of Omni's charters over the past six months," Ronan said.

"And?" Finn leaned forward, wishing he could pull all the words out of Ronan at once.

"And there were several flights to Kiev during the time you were there," Declan said. "Fleming was listed as a passenger on the flight manifest of three of them."

"Are you serious?" Finn asked, trying to make sense of the connection.

"As a heart attack," Ronan said.

Finn tugged on his beard, thinking it through. "It has to have something to do with mining right? Why else would a geologist be involved in a murder in a tiny mountain town in Ukraine?"

"That's what we're thinking," Declan said. "Ever hear anything like that while you were there?

Anything about land rights or mining rights? Any gestures by the government to take over property?"

Finn thought about it. "Not that I remember, but I wasn't involved in the business of the town. Although..."

Something snagged at his memory.

"What is it?" Elise asked.

"Fedir was in some kind of leadership position in the town." Finn had a flash of Fedir returning to the house late at night, his face drawn and tight, Iryna bringing him a glass of horilka to calm him down. "He went to town meetings a lot. Sometimes he came back... agitated."

"Agitated?" Ronan repeated.

"Like I said, I wasn't involved in that stuff," Finn said. "I tried to stay out of their business, like I always tried to stay out of the business of people I met on the road. I was there to help with the farm animals, to teach the kids some english, that was all. But I remember the meetings, remember that he didn't seem happy when he came home."

"Did you ever overhear him talking to Iryna — or anyone else — about it?" Declan asked.

"Sure," Finn said, "in Ukrainian."

"Which I take it you don't speak," Ronan said.

"Not enough to follow along when a Ukrainian native is agitated and talking to their wife."

Ronan tapped his fingers on the table. "Okay, we'll deal with it. We knew this was probably the case."

"Deal with what?" Finn asked. "Knew what was the case?"

"You're going to talk to Isaac Fleming," Elise said. "Try to get him to tell you what he knows."

Ronan looked at her. "'Talk' is an optimistic word choice."

"I didn't ask you to hurt anybody," Finn said.

"I know, which is why we're here talking to you," Ronan said. "But I have a feeling you're not ready to walk away from this. Am I wrong?"

Finn didn't have to think about his answer. He already knew Ronan was right: he just didn't like it. "No."

"That's what we figured," Declan said. "Which is why we're here."

"To give me closure?" Finn hadn't meant for his words to sound so sarcastic.

"Something like that," Ronan said.

"Wait a minute," Finn said, a new thought occurring to him. "You don't think I'll join MIS? Is that what this is about? Roping me into your enterprise?"

Anger sparked in Ronan's eyes. "Don't flatter yourself, Finn."

"Look," Declan said, "we're just trying to help. You've been gone a long time. This is important to you, and it's something we can help with. No strings attached."

Ronan still looked pissed, but Finn could tell Declan was telling the truth. "Let's say I take you up on the offer to help. What would be next?"

Declan shot a glance at Ronan before turning back to Finn. "Unless we want to tail Fleming for the foreseeable future, hoping for a break, we have to make him talk."

"How would we do that?" Finn asked.

"We grab him on his way out of the lab, take him somewhere we can work on him," Declan said.

"Work on him?" Finn repeated.

"Kick the shit out of him," Ronan said. "Make him hurt until he talks about Omni, what they're doing in Ukraine, whether they had anything to do with Fedir and Iryna's murder."

Finn shifted in his seat. Was he really considering this? Letting his brothers kidnap a scientist, beat him? "What if he doesn't talk?"

"He's a *scientist*," Declan said. "He'll talk."

"He's obviously not the muscle," Ronan

explained. "If he were, he wouldn't have been with those Blackwater assholes."

"How do you know they were part of Blackwater?"

Ronan waved away the question. "You know what I mean. Not Blackwater specifically. Some other outfit full of small-dick assholes who murder innocent people in developing countries for money."

Finn didn't go out of his way to stay on top of the news when he was traveling, but the bigger stories always made their way to his ears eventually. Technically, Blackwater didn't exist anymore. Too much bad press. But they were still alive and kicking, operating under a new name without rules in hot spots all around the world, on hire to the highest bidder.

"My money is on Fleming being some kind of consultant," Declan said. "We have Clay pulling any government docs related to land development or mining permissions, but in the meantime, I think Fleming will cave like a bad soufflé as soon as we go to work on him."

"And you're okay with that?" Elise asked. There was no judgement in her voice. It was just a question.

Ronan looked at her. "There's a lot we don't know about Fleming's involvement, but what we do know is that he stood by and watched while a bunch of armed thugs murdered a little boy's parents in their own home. And from what Finn said, he wasn't showing any remorse on his way out the door. So yeah, we're okay with giving the guy a few bruises, breaking a couple of bones if it comes to it." He turned his attention back to Finn. "So? Yes or no? I don't really give a shit either way, but if the answer is no, I'd like to go home to my wife."

"He'll live?" Finn asked. "Whatever you do to him, he'll be alive at the end of it?"

"He wouldn't be any good to us dead. He might be crawling with two broken legs, but yeah, he'll live," Ronan said.

Finn nodded. "Okay."

28

Elise ran her fingers along Finn's bare chest and nestled further into the crook of his arm. Time felt even more precious now that Ronan and Declan were back in Scotland and they had a plan for getting answers out of Isaac Fleming. Tomorrow, Finn and his brothers would stake out Fleming's lab, kidnap him, and take him to a warehouse they'd secured by the waterfront.

She had no idea what would happen after that.

She'd wondered how Finn would handle their relationship with Ronan and Declan back in the house, but nothing had changed. Finn made it clear he wanted her with him, and she'd slept in his bed each of the three nights since Ronan and Declan had returned.

She was pretty sure Ronan didn't approve, but it didn't bother her. She loved Ronan, knew he was a good man. If he had concerns, they were borne out of worry for her, but it wasn't his decision.

"Are you sure you want to go?" she asked softly, her voice a whisper in the dark.

"I wouldn't say I want to go," Finn said. "But letting Ronan and Dec handle this without me would make me a coward. I can't give them the go ahead on something like this, then close my eyes and cover my ears, pretend it's not happening."

"I get that," she said. "I'm just worried."

He tightened his arms around her and kissed her head. "You don't have to worry. There will be three of us and one of him. Declan thinks it will be quick and easy."

"Then what?" she asked. "What will you do with the information you get from Fleming?"

"Depends on what it is," Finn said.

Her eyes scanned the darkened room, only faintly lit by the streetlamp outside the window. "You're not going to take on Omni? If you find out they were part of Fedir and Iryna's death, I mean."

"I don't even know how I'd do that," Finn said. "I'm just taking it a step at a time right now."

She drew in a breath. "That's the best way. Be in

the present moment. That's what my therapist says anyway."

"Easier said than done sometimes, huh?"

She thought about the past that haunted her, the future that felt like a murky dream. "Definitely." She hesitated. "Do you think you'll be able to let it go? The thing with Fleming?"

He didn't answer right away, and she waited in the silence, giving him time to think about it.

"I haven't figured that out yet," he said. "Some of it depends on what we find out, if anything."

She knew Finn still doubted Ronan's and Declan's ability to extract information from Fleming, but Elise didn't share his doubts. They had rescued her from the most ruthless and powerful of people, people who had hidden their activities from law enforcement for years. They hadn't done it by being nice.

"I'm having trouble weighing it all out," he continued.

"Weighing what all out?" she asked.

"Justice for Petro and his parents against the necessity of doing something illegal or immoral to get it. Where does it become a perversion to call something justice? When you kidnap someone like Fleming? When you kill someone in the name of that justice? At what point is justice an excuse to do what you want to do?"

Elise turned her head to kiss his chest. She wouldn't care about him like she did if he wasn't asking these questions, questions she assumed the other Murphy brothers had asked when they started MIS.

"Have you talked to Ronan and Declan?" Elise asked.

"I'm getting the feeling they're not open to philosophical discussion," Finn said.

"Only because they've probably already had it amongst themselves," Elise said. "Maybe Nick?"

Ronan was a stoic, quietly doing what needed to be done. Declan was a hothead. He'd mellowed since he'd become a father, since he'd gotten back together with Kate, but Elise suspected there was still a part of him that enjoyed the more brutal aspects of MIS' business.

Nick was a thinker, a closet philosopher like Finn. She'd always thought that was why Nick enjoyed working the financials. It gave him time and space to contemplate the moral ambiguities of their business while fieldwork — what they called the physical missions that were usually the final part of a job — required them to take action on a moment's notice.

There was no time to philosophize the ethics of firing a gun into someone's head when they had five seconds to do it.

"Maybe," Finn said. "If it comes to it."

"I'm sorry," Elise said. "I know this is hard. I wish I had easy answers for you."

He stroked her arm. "You are the easy answer, the only thing I haven't second-guessed since I came home."

It was a rare admission, a rare acknowledgement of their relationship, which they'd both tried to enjoy without overanalyzing it.

"I feel the same way." She hesitated. She didn't want to push the boundaries of their agreement to take things as they came, but she was compelled to push them just the same. "What do you think will happen to us, when this is all over?"

He sighed, his chest rising under her ear, and she listened to the sound of his heartbeat while she waited for him to answer. "I don't know, El. I only know that I don't want it to end."

The admission should have made her happy — she didn't want it to end either — but sadness dropped into her stomach like a stone. For all their talk of being in the moment, they'd never discussed the other part of it, the part her therapist was careful to add in their sessions, a disclaimer by turns hopeful and depressing: everything ended eventually.

It wasn't a cynical view of the world — it was a realistic one. She just didn't know how to live with it, how to live with the knowledge that, like all things, her relationship with Finn would come to an end, and probably sooner rather than later.

29

Finn leaned against the building's brick exterior, his gloved hands in his pockets. Next to him, Declan blew into his own gloved hands.

"Is it ever warm here?" Declan asked.

"Sure it is, for about two weeks in the summer," Finn said.

"Great."

Finn looked at the office building across the street, his gaze sweeping the facade, looking for the light in the corner office on the tenth floor.

"See anything?" he asked into the comms system hidden in his jacket.

"Negative," Ronan said.

Finn couldn't see Ronan from where he stood, but he knew Ronan was there, watching Isaac Fleming's office and attached lab through a high-powered telescope.

"How late does this asshole work?" Declan asked.

Ronan's voice sounded in Finn's ear. "Interesting question coming from someone who comes into the office at noon."

Declan scowled. "I haven't come into the office late in months."

The dynamic between his brothers wasn't that different now than it had been when they were kids. The stakes were higher, but Ronan still led the pack, was still best at leading the pack, whether the rest of them would admit it or not. Declan was fighting to overcome his reputation as a goofball fuckup, and Nick still kept his head down, gauging which way the wind was blowing before speaking up about anything.

Finn didn't know where he stood in the grand scheme of things. It didn't really matter since he'd be gone soon anyway.

He thought of Elise and their conversation in bed the night before. They'd steered clear of their relationship in their conversations over the holiday, but that didn't mean it hadn't been on Finn's mind.

It had been on his mind too damn much.

He hadn't been surprised when Elise revealed that it had been on her mind too. What was between them — what he felt for her — was too powerful to be one-sided.

But that didn't mean he was any closer to coming up with an answer to her question. What he did know was that Isaac Fleming was in the room when Fedir and Iryna had been murdered. They'd taken Petro's parents from him. Finn couldn't focus on anything until he found out who Fleming had been working for.

"Jesus." Declan's voice was in stereo, coming both from Finn's side and from his earpiece. "I thought Fleming left the lab by eight."

"He usually does," Ronan said. "That's what the intel says anyway."

"Then what's the hold up?" Declan asked.

"Let me check my crystal ball and I'll get back to you," Ronan said.

"Fuck off," Declan said.

Ronan laughed in Finn's ear.

Their easy banter made Finn nostalgic for the relationship he'd never had with his brothers. He'd left as a kid, had grown into a man on the road. While he'd been climbing mountains and riding rickety trains across continents and working farms from Greece to Croatia, his brothers had built a business, a life, and they'd built it together.

They knew each other in ways Finn could only imagine, were close in ways that felt foreign and impossible to Finn. It filled him with melancholy even as he knew he wouldn't have changed the way he'd spent the last eight years. That was the weird thing about life: it was hard to regret anything when changing even one thing meant changing it all.

"Hold up," Ronan said.

Finn straightened. "What is it?"

It took so long for Ronan to answer, Finn thought maybe the comms system had failed. When Ronan spoke again, it was to deliver worse news than a comms failure.

"We might have a problem."

30

Elise paced the flat, then dropped onto the sofa. She picked up her glass of wine, finished it, then sat for a few seconds chewing her lip before jumping to her feet again.

This was ridiculous. She should go out, take a walk, get some food, anything to take her mind off the fact that Finn was out there with Ronan and Declan, standing in the shadows of Fleming's lab, waiting to kidnap him.

She wasn't as worried about Finn's safety as she thought she'd be. He was right: there were three of them. Fleming was one man, a scientist who, based on the background Clay had dug up, had no military training, nothing that would make him a physical threat to Finn and his brothers.

But she couldn't stop thinking about Finn's words in the dark the night before.

I'm having trouble weighing it all out...

Finn wasn't Nick or Declan. And he definitely wasn't Ronan. Elise loved her brother-in-law, loved all the Murphys. She respected them for the decision they'd made to start MIS, knew their work was based on a genuine desire to protect by removing the most dangerous people from society.

Finn hadn't made that choice. He was tough in a different way, capable of leaving behind everything he knew for the promise of something different. He'd told her about the sixteen-hour days he'd worked harvesting grapes in Italy and olives in Greece, about the time he went three days without sleeping on his way to Africa, the time he'd been grabbed by gun runners in Algeria who'd thought they might be able to get some ransom out of his family.

His moral code wasn't illustrated in shades of gray: it was black and white, right and wrong. She worried what it would do to him to watch Fleming get hurt by Ronan and Declan, and she knew he would watch, because that was the other way Finn was strong — he didn't turn his back on things that were uncomfortable, didn't give himself an easy out when things got hard. He forced himself to see things, found a way to fix what was wrong.

Except he couldn't fix this without wading into that sea of gray, and she didn't know how that would change him.

She jumped when her phone rang, then hesitated when she saw it was Julia. She thought about letting it go to voice mail, then felt ashamed. She'd been Julia's ride-or-die during more than one sleepless night when Ronan had been in the field. Her sister would never tell Ronan, but those nights were fraught with worry, about his physical safety and the possibility he would be caught and arrested and the reality that if that happened, she would have to decide whether to stay in Boston and potentially be convicted as an accomplice to MIS' business, leaving JT an orphan, or whether she would take the fake identities Ronan had set up for them all and run.

Now Julia was worrying because of Finn, because Ronan and Declan were doing Finn a favor.

"Hey," Elise said into the phone.

"Hey," Julia said. Elise waited for her sister to vent, but when she spoke, her voice was a little breathless, like she had something important to say. "What was the name of that company that took over Fringe?"

"Hi, Jules. I'm great, totally fine waiting to find out if the guy I'm seeing has been arrested or if his psyche has been permanently damaged. Thanks for asking. How are you?"

Julia sighed. "I'm sorry. We'll get to that stuff in a sec. Can you just answer the question? Please?"

Elise thought back to the research she'd done on William Pearson when Bonnie told her and Aliyah about the sale of the store. "Mirage Holdings? I think that's it."

"That's what I thought," Julia said. "You're not going to believe this, El."

An alarm had started ringing somewhere in Elise's mind. "What?"

"The company Isaac Fleming is working for? The Omni Group?"

"Yeah?"

"They're the parent company for Mirage Holdings, among others," Julia said.

"Wait... are you saying the company Isaac Fleming is doing work for is the same company that now owns Fringe?" Elise asked.

"That's what I'm saying."

Elise paced to the flat's big living room window, trying to process what Julia was saying. It was less than a week after the holidays, and the city remained festively lit and decorated. If it was anything like Boston, in another week it would all be gone, the formerly magical city suddenly turning gray and dirty.

"It has to be a coincidence right?" Elise said. There was no way the purchase of Fringe was connected to whatever Isaac Fleming was up to with the Omni Group. What would be the motivation? Fringe was a small, single-location store like a million others across the country.

And it's not like anyone could have known about Elise's relationship to Finn. It hadn't even existed back when Bonnie sold the store.

"I don't know," Julia said. "Probably? When did Bonnie sell the store?"

"A couple months ago."

"You weren't even with Finn back then," Julia said.

"Exactly. So why does it sound like this worries you?" Elise asked.

Julia sighed. "I've been here before, that's all."

"Where's here?"

"The place where pieces look like they should fit together but don't, and then later you find out your gut was right, they do fit together, but in ways you hadn't imagined."

Elise wondered if her sister was talking about Manifest, about the months it had taken her and Ronan to find Elise, tracking her across multiple countries and three continents.

"What do we do?" Elise asked.

"Right now? We wait for Ronan, Dec, and Finn to finish the job with Isaac Fleming, see what they turn up. Then we dig deeper into this connection until it either leads nowhere or leads somewhere," Julia said.

"Great." Elise couldn't imagine it leading somewhere, couldn't imagine the sale of Fringe connected in any way to a multinational corporation who might have ordered the murder of two innocent people in a Ukrainian village.

Then again, she couldn't have imagined that she'd be standing in Scotland, waiting for her lover to return from a mission to beat a man for information on that murder either.

Her life looked nothing like what it had looked like before Finn Murphy.

Julia was right. All they could do was wait. The notion infuriated her. Was that what had prompted Julia to spend her nights looking for Elise after she'd gone missing? Was that what had prompted her to lurk in the alley behind Seth's house, watching for any sign of Elise, all the men around her telling her they would take care of it, that they would find Elise, while days turned into weeks and Elise remained missing?

Elise understood it, but she wasn't her sister. Julia was smart and logical, determined and methodical. If Julia resolved to fix something, it got fixed, one way or another.

Elise had never had Julia's drive or initiative. There had been a time when she'd been proud of their differences, proud of her spontaneous streak and her focus on enjoying all that life had to offer.

Now she wanted to have something to offer, to help Finn in a way that mattered. She wanted him to have closure, to move on with his life in peace, even if it wasn't with her.

She sighed. It was a pointless endeavor. She was just a sales clerk. What could she possibly to to help?

31

"Four men just exited the elevator on Fleming's floor," Ronan said.

Declan met Finn's eyes as he answered into the comms system. "So?"

"Let's just say they don't look like tax auditors," Ronan said.

Declan scowled. "What does that — "

Ronan cut him off. "On my way."

Declan cursed.

"What's happening?" Finn immediately regretted the question. He knew what was *happening*, but he didn't know what it meant.

"Fuck if I know," Declan said. "You know Ronan. He'll tell us when he tells us."

Finn paced in the shadows until Declan told him

to stop, that he was drawing attention to them. By the time Ronan sprinted across the street, Finn's nerves were strung tight.

"What the fuck is happening?" he asked. Ronan was already drawing his weapon. "And why do you have your gun out?"

"We have to go in." Ronan started for the side of the building. "Those guys didn't come through the lobby. I was watching. And they look like they mean business."

Finn was frozen in place as Declan started after Ronan. "Hired help?"

"Looks like it," Ronan said.

"One of you assholes better tell me what's going on," Finn said.

Declan stopped. "Looks like our friends at the Omni Group might have decided Fleming is a loose end they can't afford. Bad dudes are on their way into the lab. If you want answers out of Fleming, we have to get to him before they do."

Adrenaline flooded Finn's body. This wasn't part of the plan.

Ronan looked at him. "You don't have to come. You can go home and wait. We got this."

Petro's face swam in Finn's mind, the boy's sad

eyes when he'd said goodbye to Finn telling the story of all that had been taken from him.

Finn sprinted forward with his brothers.

He didn't ask how Ronan knew the security code to get them in through the service entrance. He didn't ask how Ronan had been prepared with face masks or why he and Declan had brought guns when they were supposed to shove Fleming in the SUV with tinted windows that had shown up outside the flat that morning.

There was no time, and Finn's gut told him they'd skidded through the stop sign of the mostly-safe-but-still-illegal plan of kidnapping Fleming into something that was also illegal but a hell of a lot more dangerous.

The mask felt strange on Finn's face as they moved quickly through the service area at the back of the building, a nondescript factory room lined with packages and cleaning supplies. Overhead, fluorescent lighting buzzed, casting the room in a weak blue light, making the building look like a warehouse from a horror movie instead of one of Aberdeen's quaint old buildings.

The light made Finn nervous. It meant service staff was still in the building working, security maybe, or the cleaning crew.

He hurried behind Ronan and in front of Declan, understanding they assumed this formation because Finn was the weak link in their chain, that his brothers were protecting him. It wasn't a feeling he enjoyed, but he didn't have time to examine it.

They entered a narrow stairwell (how had Ronan known where it was?) and Finn followed Ronan up the stairs, careful to keep his footsteps silent when he noticed Ronan walking carefully on the treads.

They circled around the landing for the second floor, the third, the fourth.

It had begun to feel like a nightmare, the one where you're at the end of a long tunnel but no matter how fast you run it never ends, when they reached the landing to the tenth floor.

Ronan flattened his back against the wall next to the door. Declan did the same on the other side, tugging on Finn's jacket, forcing him to follow suit.

Ronan put a finger to his lips and pointed at the door.

Declan's voice filled the comms system at a whisper. "Stay behind Ronan. Do exactly what we say."

Ronan reached for the door leading to the tenth floor and pulled.

He looked through the opening and waved Finn forward. Declan was at his back as he stepped into a shadowed hallway, most of the lights turned out for the night. Closed doors lined the hall, all of them with identifying placards: Lab 3E, Lab 3F, Decontamination #2.

Ronan moved silently down the hall. Finn followed, careful not to let his shoes squeak on the linoleum floor. As they made their way past the rooms, Finn saw that some of them were fronted with windows giving a view into rooms filled with long metal tables, steel refrigerators with temperature gauges on the front, microscopes lined up like soldiers waiting to be deployed.

The rooms were empty, dark except for the indicator lights of the equipment inside, and Finn followed Ronan to the end of the hall, stopping when Ronan paused to listen before rounding the corner.

Finn trained his ears to the silence and didn't hear anything but the faint hum of the lab's equipment, toiling away in the dark.

Finn looked at Declan and lifted his eyebrows.

"Too quiet," Dec whispered.

Finn's stomach tightened into a knot. He hadn't had time to be nervous before now. His adrenaline had kept him moving, focused on being quiet, on not making a mistake, on following Ronan's lead.

But now, in the silence of the lab, he realized they had no idea what they were walking into. Isaac Fleming was working somewhere nearby. Ronan had seen a group of men step off the elevator onto this floor.

That was all they knew.

And Declan was right. It was too quiet. Finn felt it in his bones even if he didn't know why it was a problem.

Ronan waved them forward and they eased farther down the hall. Up ahead, light spilled out into the hall through one of the lab windows, casting a rectangle onto the shadowed linoleum a few feet in front of them.

Fleming's lab. It had to be.

Finn followed Ronan to the edge of the window, where he stopped and stood back against the wall. Ronan looked at Declan and lifted his hand, his fingers running through a series of signals. He turned to Finn, his gaze lingering on Finn's face.

Finn immediately understood the true ramifications of his presence. He didn't understand their hand signals, didn't know how to fire a gun, didn't even have a gun on him.

His brothers had come here to help him, and now they were in danger because of him.

Ronan looked back at Declan. Everything Finn needed to know was in Declan's answering shrug.

They were here now. They'd have to do the best they could.

Ronan drew in a breath and leaned in, peering through the window in the door before turning the knob.

Finn stepped into the room behind him, his eyes sweeping the space, his mind instinctively trying to get a handle on the environment they were stepping into. It was a series of impressions: steel and glass and microscopes and slides, no refrigerators here, but chisels and picks and other instruments that might have belonged in a mining operation if they'd been bigger and dirtier.

These instruments gleamed under the lab's lights. Chips of stones in varying sizes were lined up on one of the metal tables. A man in a lab coat stood at one of them, his back to the door as he leaned over a microscope.

Finn made a second sweep of the room, but there was no sign of anyone else.

Ronan raised his weapon and pointed it at the back of the man's head. When he spoke, his voice was low, almost conversational. "Stop what you're doing and put your hands in the air. Now."

The man froze, something clattering onto the table in front of him.

Finn glanced at Declan and was surprised to find his eyes not on Fleming, but scanning the room like Finn had done.

Looking for the other men, the ones Ronan had seen through the telescope across the street.

When Finn looked back at Fleming, the man's empty hands were in the air.

"Turn around. Nice and slow," Ronan said.

Fleming did, and Finn was met with a jolt of recognition. In this setting, Fleming looked harmless, a small-framed man with a receding hairline of mousy brown hair, glasses perched on the end of a thin nose.

His eyes told a different story. They were too bright, too defiant given the situation.

"On your knees," Ronan said, removing a set of zip ties from his pocket.

Fleming held his hands out in front of him, the gesture submissive even if the light in his eyes was anything but. "Whatever you want, I'm sure we can discuss it like —"

Finn almost didn't register why Fleming didn't finish his sentence. Glass exploded around the room, a series of gunshots ringing off the metal equipment as Declan shoved Finn to the ground.

Finn face-planted on the linoleum, his mind spinning as he tried to grasp the activity around him: Declan crouched and skirting one side of the room, looking for another angle on the intruders, Ronan flipping one of the metal tables, using it as cover as he fired on the black-clad men who had barreled, guns blazing, through the door at the other end of the room.

Like them, the men wore face masks and carried weapons. Unlike them, these men wore Kevlar, carried semiautomatics, and moved into the room with focused authority.

They didn't care if they made noise.

And around all of this — the shattering glass and the gunfire that made Finn's ears ring and the clang of equipment falling off tables as the men advanced into the room — Finn saw an arm clad in a white lab coat, flung out with the palm turned toward the ceiling behind one of the metal tables along the wall where Fleming had been working.

Finn crawled toward it, trying to stay behind the metal tables as the gunfire died down, his brothers firing off an occasional round while the men trying to kill them — the ones who were left — filled the air with the sporadic stutter of their weapons.

Finn rounded the corner of the metal table and looked at the man lying facedown on the linoleum.

No, no, no...

He turned Isaac Fleming onto his back and looked at the seeping red stain blossoming on the chest of his lab coat. Fleming blinked, still alive.

Finn grabbed the front of his lab coat and lifted his body a few inches off the floor. "Who hired you to go to the village in Ukraine?"

"Village...?" The man sputtered, and a stream of blood emerged from the side of his mouth. "Which one?"

"Which one?" The question took Finn's breath away. "The one where you killed Fedir and Iryna Kolisnyk? Where you murdered them in their home? Who were you working for?"

Fleming's mouth opened and closed, like a fish out of water. Something gurgled inside his throat as he tried to form a word.

"Tell me, dammit." Finn leaned closer, placing his ear near Fleming's blood-stained lips.

"Black..." Fleming sputtered again. "Ridge..."

Finn strained to hear, but nothing else emerged from Fleming's lips. When he looked into the man's face, he saw why: Fleming's eyes were wide open, staring sightless at the ceiling.

"Is he dead?"

Finn looked up to see Ronan standing over him. He didn't look like he'd broken a sweat.

"He's dead," Finn said. He registered the silence in the room and stood to look for Declan, relieved when he saw his other brother rifling through the vests of the dead mercenaries who'd killed Isaac Fleming.

Somewhere in the distance, sirens rang through the night, their peal growing closer.

"What now?" Finn asked.

Ronan shoved him toward the door. "Now we get the fuck out of here."

Finn didn't look back.

32

Elise watched Fringe come into view as Finn navigated around the corner. He turned off the car and she looked at the store's window across the street. Behind the glass, three mannequins posed atop fake snow, all dressed in a suitable if generic array of winter clothing.

Her heart sank a little. The vignette lacked Aliyah's usual flair, something that was undoubtedly a product of Aliyah's newly limited choice in inventory.

"It is weird being back?" Finn asked.

She turned to look at him, and her breath caught in her throat. She couldn't believe he was hers, for now at least. "Yeah," she said. "Is it weird for you?"

"No weirder than it was the first time."

She nodded. Finn had a lot of experience moving around. "What are you going to do today?"

He turned his gaze to the windshield, his eyes fixed on something outside. "Going into the office for a bit, see if Clay has turned up anything new."

"Keep me posted?" she asked.

They had no idea what Isaac Fleming's last words meant, if anything. They'd only been back a couple of days, the situation in Scotland a mess that was being cleaned up by local authorities. News coverage had been sparse, limited to brief mentions by Scottish news outlets of a lab break-in and murder.

She'd been worried at first, worried the police would come knocking, looking for Finn, Ronan, and Declan. But they'd worn gloves, and other than the security footage which would show them entering the building in ski masks, they'd been careful not to leave any trace of their presence.

Ronan believed that after seeing the security footage the police would focus on the men who had killed Isaac Fleming, not on the others who'd been present as witnesses.

"I better go in." She leaned in to kiss Finn. "See you at five?"

His lips lingered on her own, the passion that

always simmered between them pulsing under the tenderness of his kiss. "I can't wait."

She smiled against his lips. "Me neither."

She opened the car door before she changed her mind. She'd never wanted less to be on her way into Fringe.

She closed the door and waited for a car to pass before hurrying across the street. It was as cold in Boston as it had been in Scotland, but the cold felt more ominous here, a harbinger of the danger they were in now that the people behind Fleming's murder knew they'd been witness to it.

After today, she wouldn't be immune. It had taken every ounce of persuasion to convince Julia not to tell Ronan and his brothers about the connection between Mirage Holdings and the Omni Group. Elise had played on all her sister's weak spots — her love for Elise, Julia's experience trying to find her when everyone told her to leave it alone, her determination to contribute when everyone else was content to let her wring her hands on the sidelines.

There was some logic to Elise's argument — Julia had found nothing to indicate that the connection between Mirage and Omni was anything other than a coincidence — but in the end, it had been Elise's personal appeal that had tipped Julia to her side.

Julia still didn't like it, and she'd made no bones about the fact that if things changed, if a meaningful connection was found between Omni and the sale of Fringe to one of their subsidiaries, she would go to Ronan in a heartbeat, but she'd agreed to keep it between them for the time being.

Elise felt bad putting her sister in such an awkward position, a position Elise understood all too well since she hadn't told Finn about the connection either, but they would both have to live with the guilt for a little while.

She opened the door to the store and stepped inside, unraveling her scarf as she looked around, taking in the store's new layout — designed to mimic other stores in the Mirage family — and merchandise.

It was a strange mix of the familiar and foreign. It still smelled like Fringe, and the winter light still streamed in the front window in the same way, but the new layout and inventory made it feel like she'd walked into a familiar room to find the furniture had been rearranged.

"Hello."

She looked up to find William Pearson staring at her from the door to the back room. "Morning. Is Aliyah here?"

"No." The answer was terse, but she didn't know William Pearson well enough to know whether it was because it was just his way or whether he was pissed she'd been gone so long.

Fear rippled through her at another possibility: that William Pearson knew what had happened in Scotland, that he knew about what had happened in Ukraine and knew about her relationship with Finn.

She forced herself to breathe. She was being crazy, letting her anxiety run away with her.

She started taking off her coat, and she was surprised when William came toward her and helped her remove it. He was too close, close enough that she felt his breath on her neck. It sent a shiver up her spine, and not in a good way.

"Thanks," she said.

He handed her the coat. "Welcome back."

His suit looked like it had just been pressed, his face freshly shaved, short hair trimmed and neat. For all intents and purposes, he should have been harmless, especially compared to Finn's wildness.

So why did Elise feel scared?

She nodded. "I guess I better get to work."

She moved past him and headed for the back room. She didn't know how — or even if — her job at Fringe would help uncover Omni's involvement in

Fedir and Iryna's murder, but for now, it made sense to keep the channel open. She would use her access to the company, see what she could turn up.

Finn wouldn't be hers forever, but while he was, she would do whatever she could to help him, to set him free from what had happened in Ukraine. She would hold him tight, memorize everything about him.

And if goodbye came — when it came — she would be grateful for every moment.

33

Finn watched Elise as she crossed the street and opened the door to the store. Why did it feel like his heart was in his throat every time she left him?

They'd fled Scotland in a hurry after Fleming's murder. Thanks to Ronan and Declan, they'd covered their bases at the lab, making it impossible for anyone to know they'd been there when Fleming was killed, but there was no reason to push their luck.

They'd spent the last two days resting at the house and acclimating to the time change, but now it was time to get to work. Finn had only considered letting Fedir and Iryna's murder go for about ten seconds before he realized it wasn't an option.

He couldn't live with it, couldn't live with himself,

especially not when he knew the Omni Group was involved. He didn't know how — not yet — but that they were involved at all was too reminiscent of all the things that were wrong in the world: corporate greed and corruption, the rich getting richer while the people who did the real work, the people who toiled in factories and on farms, got poorer and poorer, increasingly seen as tools to be used by their corporate overlords rather than human beings deserving of safe working conditions and a living wage.

He may not know why Omni was involved in Fedir and Iryna's murders, but they were dead, so it was safe to say Omni's involvement wasn't altruistic.

He watched Elise walk into the store on the other side of the glass. She paused, and he thought she must be talking to someone. A moment later, a man in a suit came into view.

William Pearson, Elise's new boss. It had to be.

Finn watched as he reached to help Elise with her coat. Was it Finn's imagination that he stood too close? Closer than was appropriate for a boss and employee?

The knot in his gut tightened, and he was surprised to find that he was gripping the steering wheel of Julia's car so tightly that his knuckles had gone white.

Elise disappeared from view and he started the car and pulled out into the street.

He took a few deep breaths, tried to calm the adrenaline moving through his body, too close to anger to be called anything else.

It was completely irrational. He didn't own Elise. It wasn't his business if someone got too close to her, unless that person was a danger to her.

Then it would very much be his business.

Still, he couldn't deny that the sight of another man so close to her had pissed him off. He didn't have a right, and it didn't make sense, but there it was.

Twenty minutes after leaving Fringe he pulled next to Ronan's car in a mostly empty parking lot on the outskirts of town. It was cold enough to see his breath as he made his way inside a warehouse building at the age of the lot, and he had a sudden longing to be back in Scotland, to be alone with Elise in the flat, her naked body against his, the smell of her hair in his nose and on his pillow.

They'd slept together every night since they'd been home, but it wasn't the same as having her to himself, as the two of them being alone, feeling like the only people on the planet.

Would they ever have that again? He didn't know.

He pulled open a wooden door and stepped inside a shabby room with linoleum flooring. Guns lined the walls along with assorted ammunition, and gunfire echoed down a long hall with a door at the end.

"You're late," Ronan said, walking toward him.

"Traffic," Finn said.

Ronan handed him a weapon. "It's empty. We're going to start at the beginning."

The weapon was oddly light in Finn's hand given its bulk. It could have been a toy, but it wasn't. It was real, and Finn was really doing this.

He was doing it because he never wanted to be the weak link again, never wanted to rely on his brothers — or anyone else — to protect him ever again.

Most of all, he wanted to be able to protect the people that mattered to him. Whatever happened in the future, he would never again stand by and let someone hurt the people he loved.

"You ready to get started?" Ronan asked.

Elise's face flashed in front of his eyes and his

chest swelled with emotion. It wasn't entirely welcome. It was messy and complicated and uncertain, all the things he'd spent eight years avoiding.

But it was there. It was real.

He nodded and followed his brother down the hall to the firing range.

Thank you for reading Coming Home! Finn and Elise's story continues in Home Turf. Find out what happens when the power behind Issac Fleming is revealed - and the deadly consequences to Finn and Elise are brought home to Boston.

Did you enjoy this book? Please help other readers find it by leaving a review.

Join the Michelle St. James email list at www.michellestjames.com for book news and freebies - never more than once a month!

Please find me online. I'd love to get to know you!

Facebook: Michelle St James
Twitter: MStJames_Author
Instagram: Michelle St. James
Bookbub: Michelle St. James
Syndicate Sinners Facebook Reader Group

ALSO BY MICHELLE ST. JAMES

Ruthless

Fearless

Lawless

Muscle

Savage

Primal

Eternal

Covenant

Revenant

Rule

The Sentinel

Rogue Love

Rebel Love

Fire with Fire

Into the Fire

Through the Fire

Eternal Love

King of Sin

Wages of Sin

The Awakening of Nina Fontaine

The Surrender of Nina Fontaine

The Liberation of Nina Fontaine

Thicker Than Water

Blood in the Water

Hell or High Water

Murphy's Law

Murphy's Wrath

Murphy's Love

Wicked Game

Fair Game

End Game

Printed in Great Britain
by Amazon